PATROL

PATROL

by
Philip Macdonald

CASEMATE
uk
Oxford & Philadelphia

Published in Great Britain and
the United States of America in 2016 by
CASEMATE PUBLISHERS
10 Hythe Bridge Street, Oxford OX1 2EW, UK
and

1950 Lawrence Road, Havertown, PA 19083, USA

© Philip Macdonald 1927

Paperback Edition: ISBN 978-1-61200-378-8
Digital Edition: ISBN 978-1-61200-379-5

A CIP record for this book is available from the British Library

Printed in the Czech Republic by FINIDR.

For a complete list of Casemate titles, please contact:

CASEMATE PUBLISHERS (UK)
Telephone (01865) 241249
Fax (01865) 794449
Email: casemate-uk@casematepublishers.co.uk
www.casematepublishers.co.uk

CASEMATE PUBLISHERS (US)
Telephone (610) 853-9131
Fax (610) 853-9146
Email: casemate@casematepublishing.com
www.casematepublishing.com

TO

THE OTHER RANKS

OF

1914–1918

CAST OF CHARACTERS

Abelson

Brown

Cook

Corporal Bell

Hale

MacKay

Morelli

Pearson

Sanders

The Sergeant

PATROL

I

"I DON'T exactly know," said the Sergeant half aloud, "what to do with him."

The head which rested on his knee shifted a little and a froth of blood bubbled suddenly at the corners of the mouth.

"'M!" said the Sergeant. "Bell!"

The Corporal who stood beside him knelt, peering at the face on the Sergeant's knee. "That's that" he said.

The Sergeant freed his right hand and groped under the boy's tunic. He looked as if he were listening. Presently his fingers came away. He said:

"Yes. Pity. Decent boy in some ways. No soldier." He gently eased down the body until it lay flat upon the sand. He dried his hand upon the side of his breeches and began methodically to empty the pockets of the body's drill tunic.

The Corporal rose to his feet and dusted the soft grey-dun sand from his right leg. "There's those entrenching tools," he said. "Will I get two-three o' the blokes to start in?"

"Yes," said the Sergeant. He did not look up; he was arranging the contents of the dead subaltern's pockets in small heaps, tidily.

Corporal Bell turned and walked slowly, with his lounging gait, back over the twenty yards which separated the body of their officer from the eight troopers who made up the rest of this small patrol. These stood and sat in a listless group. Over an arm of each man were the reins of his horse, standing above and beside him. Both men and horses seemed to droop a little: it was as if the sun which beat down upon them had weighted rays which were pressing them towards the sand.

The Corporal came up to this group. He said:

"Morelli, Pearson, Brown—hand over your goras to Hale, put your rifles back in the buckets an' get those three entrenching tools."

Three men rose and gave their reins to a fourth, who now disappeared within a shifting ring of horses, out from which his voice, nasal and Cockney, rose ever and again in bitter, plaintive obscenity.

"What's on, Corp?" A giant of a man emerged from the cluster. In his hand was a small, oddly-shaped spade. He looked at it, turning it this way and that. "What's on?" he repeated.

"Muriel's got his," said the Corporal, "clean through left lung." He raised his voice. "Come on, you two, Brown's here. What *you* playin' about at? Jildi!"

They came; two small men: Pearson shuffling, despondent, beads of sweat running down his face from beneath his topee. Morelli stocky, alert, cheerful.

The Corporal surveyed the three. "Fall in, Sextons," he said. "Come on!" He led the way.

"What's on?" Morelli cocked his head to look up at Brown. "We gotta make nice comfort'ble bed for His Majesty's Second Lif'tenant A. de C. G. Hawkins?"

"Comfort hell!" Brown said. "He's out."

"What's that?" Pearson raised his drawn little face.

Brown looked down at him. "Muriel," he said, "is napoo. The officer is dead. Our commander is no longer alive. We are grave-diggers. Understand now, Pansy?"

"Oh! shut up!" Pearson muttered. He plodded on, shoulders bent.

"Bleeding queer, that Buddo suddenly poppin' up like that!" Morelli raised a hand and tilted his topee forward to scratch at the back of his head. "Where'd the bleeder *come* from?"

"I nearly got him with my second," said Brown. "Damn' fast that horse was, though. But he was a good shot. Bell says right through Muriel's left lung." He fell silent as they came up to the Sergeant and the body at his feet.

"Whereabouts?" asked the Corporal.

"Anywhere. Anywhere. Only get busy." The Sergeant was preoccupied. He held a map outspread before him.

The sand was loose. The three sweated. There was presently a hole pronounced by the Corporal as of sufficient depth. Into this was placed the body of Second-Lieutenant (acting Lieutenant) Arthur de Courcy Grammont Hawkins.

"Get on! Get on!" said the Sergeant.

The three entrenching tools and the boots of the Corporal swept back the sand.

"Going to mark it?" the Corporal asked.

The Sergeant shook his head. "What's the good?" He came close and surveyed their work. "Stamp it down a bit," he said.

They stamped it down.

The Sergeant looked again. He said:

"That'll do. Bell, get 'em mounted." He unfolded the map again. "Bring my mare along, Morelli."

Three minutes later the little party, riding two abreast but with ten yards or so between each couple, moved off again, heading almost due north. Already loose sand had drifted over the stamped-down square which momentarily had distinguished the subaltern's grave: now there was no sign, no mark, no indication whatsoever. There had been, here, eleven men. Now ten rode away. A man had been cancelled.

II

THEY had been marching for an hour—ten minutes' trot, fifteen minutes' walk, five minutes' rest.

After the second rest, as they trotted, the Sergeant, ahead, turned in his saddle.

"Corporal Bell!" he called.

The Corporal cantered from his place until he rode level. "Yes," he said.

For several moments the Sergeant was silent. At last he said, looking straight ahead of him:

"Know where we are, Bell?"

"No," said the Corporal.

The Sergeant turned now. "Know what we were meant to do, Bell?"

"No," said the Corporal.

"Neither do I." He laughed a little.

"Eh!" said Bell, in a startled voice.

"You heard me," said the Sergeant. He jerked his head to indicate the place where the subaltern had been buried. "That young fool! He never told me his orders."

"*What?*" Bell said, and sat upright in his saddle.

The Sergeant shook his head. "Not a word; not a mutter. I asked him, four or five times. It was always: 'Yes, yes, Sergeant; I must do that.' Last time he said: 'To-morrow.' *To-morrow!*" He cleared his throat and spat savagely into the sand. "To-morrow! Well, here's our to-morrow! Nice one, too! Isn't it?"

The Corporal rubbed at his unshaven chin, rasping the strap of his helmet up and down against the blue stubble. "Where're we heading now?" he asked.

"I've worked it out," the Sergeant said, "as best I can. We're goin' dead north. We ought to hit the river by to-morrow night. That is, assumin' I'm somewhere near right about where we were when that young fool pegged out."

"We may hit the river," Bell said slowly. "And that'll be that? But what else'll we hit?"

The Sergeant hunched his shoulders; barely a shrug. "Search me!" he said. "It's a fine thing—a patrol patrollin' without known' what they're at. An' the orders locked up in that dead brat. They ought to have 'em on paper. They would in a real army. But here am I: I know the Brigade was movin' yesterday after we left 'em; I know we were to join 'em. But I *don't* know which way they were goin', *or* where we were to strike up with 'em."

The Corporal's lips pursed themselves in a soundless whistle. He rubbed at his chin again but did not speak.

The two rode on in silence unbroken for perhaps five minutes.

"Don't say anything," said the Sergeant at last, "to the men. Not yet." He held up his arm, easing his horse to a walk. The narrow double line, spread thinly out behind him, ceased jigging.

Almost at once, with the change, came a thinning of the separate clouds of dusty sand which had enveloped each couple. Brown, riding as first file with Morelli, scrubbed at his lips, first with his naked forearm, then, more usefully, with a foul but at least not sand-covered handkerchief. "Thank God!" he said.

"Ah," Morelli agreed. "An' a gink can't even spit. Christ! I'm dry." He spoke with the faintest traces of an American accent, born of those nine months in 1913 when, as the senior and male half of Morel and Moree, he had danced in the lesser vaudeville theatres of New York, Chicago, and Pittsburg.

"What about a swig?" Brown spoke doubtfully, feeling with tentative fingers at the string of his water-bottle cork.

"Shouldn't," said Morelli.

"'Spose not." Brown reluctantly lifted his hand back to the reins again.

Both men, on a common train of thought, turned to look behind them. There, ten yards away, rode Hale. He had no companion, but led a spare horse across whose back was a pack-saddle of curious shape: at each side of this saddle, below other cases, was strapped a long leather case like a bolster.

"We're windy!" Morelli said.

"Oy!" called Hale. "Wot yer worryin' abaht? Fink I've drunk it all!"

"—!" said Brown. He smiled. Every one smiled with Hale the military as they had with Hale the prosperous fish-hawker.

The quarter-hour came to its end. Again the Sergeant flung up his arm, this time halting his horse. The files closed up to him and to each other.

They dismounted, to form such another group as that of an hour before. They had travelled perhaps eight miles; but this, for all the change in their surrounding, might have been less than ten yards.

"Might's well be on the shifting platform at the Lane!" Abelson looked about him, his leering Semite mouth curled in disgust, "Ride, ride, ride, and bleeding well ride. *And* ride. And nothing to show for it! I says— it! *And* — it!" He did not repeat himself. — the war! And — the bleeding day *I* joined up! — it *all*!"

Sanders, who had been sitting with his head in his hands, looked up wearily. He said:

"That foul tongue of yours is a public offence, Abelson." He spoke English with an accent whose purity would have been remarkable at a dinner of The Pedants: coming from the unshaven lips of an unkept trooper in the British Army it was so incongruous as to be almost an indecency.

Abelson, who was standing, wheeled round to look down at his attacker. He hunched his shoulders, and his heavy jowl, covered with black stubble, was thrust forward. His eyes closed to slits. The fingers of his right hand bunched themselves into a fist at the end of a heavily-muscled forearm. He said:

"Yeh praying, oily, bahstud!"

His tone was an offence greater than the words. Sanders' thin, high-nosed face showed the rush of blood even beneath the tan and beard and sweat-caked dust. But he closed tighter his thin lips.

"Yeh—!" said Abelson, bending. "Yeh bloody offal!"

"Put a sock in it!" Brown said wearily from beside the two. "Leave the feller alone, Abelson."

"Leave him alone! Leave him alone?" growled the Jew. "Why don't he leave *me*? He's *asking* for a poke in the ear! Beggin' for it." He looked down at Sanders again, and into Sanders' bright, mad eyes of pale and blazing blue.

"Aren't yeh?" Abelson said. "I'm sick of yeh! Every time I open me mouth, *you* chip in. And I've told yeh what's coming. Haven't I now?"

Sanders climbed stiffly to his feet; a man of medium height and uncertain age, thin and meagre and stooping. In the Regiment's records his civil occupation was shown enigmatically as "student."

"I'm here," he said. "Hit me if you wish."

The Sergeant's voice came from behind him suddenly. "Saunders! Take that rifle of yours off your saddle. And you, too, Abelson and Hale. You'll all be in trouble if you're not careful."

These three turned to their horses and each from a long bucket on the off side drew his rifle. The Sergeant passed on.

At the rear fringe of the group, its penultimate file, Pearson sat alone. Looped round his right arm were the reins of two horses, for to him had fallen the lot of leading the dead subaltern's charger. The Corporal had told him as if he were conferring an honour... Damn him! the great hulking swine! Why didn't he lead the horse himself? Bad enough to ride that mare he'd got, which would jig-jig all the time, even when they were at the walk...

His throat was parched and aching, his mouth full of grit, his tongue stiff and unmanageable. He tried to straighten his bowed shoulders, but the weight and hardness of the laden bandolier seemed suddenly to have increased unbearably, so that, in spite of the heat, he almost wished that his drill tunic were over his shirt rather than, like all the others, with the Regiment's transport.

He felt with sly fingers for his water-bottle. He looked cautiously round him. None of the others... how did they manage not to... His hand felt the weight of the cloth-covered bottle; its leather traps and metal neck scorched his fingers. The bottle was light. Too light. He should not have used so much. Presently it would be empty.

Well, Presently would look after itself. He swung the bottle round to the front of his body. The charger chose this moment to shift away, thus pulling at his right arm.

"*Come* up!" whined Pearson, and jerked at its mouth. He got both hands to the bottle and started to ease the cork.

"Pearson!" said the Sergeant's voice.

"Sergeant?" He got somehow to his feet, slipping the bottle again to its place at his side.

The Sergeant faced him and put out a hand and weighed the bottle in his palm. He said:

"You're a fool, Pearson."

"Yes, Sergeant."

"Take it off and give it to me."

The little man hesitated: he would, he felt, sooner have obeyed an order to cut off one of his fingers.

"Look slippy!" the Sergeant said. "*I* shan't drink it, y'know. And then you'll have more to-night."

"Yes, Sergeant." He slipped the strap from his shoulder and held out the bottle. The Sergeant took it and passed on.

He came, last, to Cook and MacKay, the inseparables. Cook, sitting, held two rifles embraced by one enormous arm upon which showed dully, through the coated dust, the crude colours of a tattooed snake. Standing with the two horses was MacKay. He held a very small piece of sponge, drenched from his water-bottle, and with this was wiping the caked filth from the nostrils of his chestnut.

The Sergeant stood watching. MacKay, the nostrils done, slipped the reins of Cook's black up over his arm, and, with both hands thus free, opened the chestnut's mouth and scrubbed with the damp sponge at the gums and tongue and roof. He stopped, releasing the lower jaw. The horse pushed its head against the man's shoulder, then fumbled with caressing lips at his ear.

"Ye great carrl!" said MacKay gently. He turned to Cook. "Matlow," he said, and held out the sponge. "Ye just gi' yon a drop out ye' boatle."

"Ar," Cook said. He took the sponge, held it over the neck of his bottle, and shook water on to it.

MacKay repeated his work upon the black. When he had finished, the Sergeant spoke.

"It does brighten 'em up," he said.

"Ay." MacKay took his rifle from Cook's arm, slung it by its webbing band over his shoulder, and surveyed the two horses. They stood noticeably more alert than their fellows. Their heads hung, but not with such utter dejection. They had not, now, that appearance of being upon the point of lying in the sand. "Ay," said MacKay again. "'F there waur ony ither so'jers heere, horrses wud a' be like yon." He tilted back his topee and wiped at the sweat on his forehead with his forearm: the action showed the white hair at his temples and the radiating mesh of wrinkles about his bloodshot eyes. He added: "So they wud, too, 'f Ah waur in charrge."

The Sergeant smiled. "That's all right, Jock," he said. MacKay was privileged. Once, half-way back through his twenty-five years' pre-war service, he had been a Squadron-Sergeant-Major. But whisky, at first in easy steps, then with a rushing slide, had brought him low again. He left the army a trooper, as a trooper he enlisted in this regiment when war broke out. A trooper he was still, having steadfastly refused many offers of promotion.

"What's a'right?" he said.

The Sergeant laughed. "About the horses. Next halt, they'll be watered. I want you to do it, MacKay. Third of a bucket each, or a little less. That right-hand bag mustn't be touched. Get me?"

MacKay nodded. "Ay."

"But first you'll draw just a drop from the bag and take it round. They'll all be sponged out before watering."

"Ay."

"Right. Start in the minute we halt next time." The Sergeant turned on his heel and walked back to where Morelli held his horse.

The patrol mounted and rode on. It was early afternoon and with every minute the sun impossibly grew hotter. They were trotting, and the forty-eight hooves raised each its cloud of grey dust, soft yet gritty. These clouds flew high and joined themselves until around each couple, always with them, enveloping, hung a foul veil in which sight was difficult, speech impossible, and life itself an irksome discomfort. The grey powder hung to their skin, their hair, their clothes: horses and men were dingy, sweating ghosts.

III

THEY first saw it between three and four o'clock that afternoon.

"Bell!" The Sergeant pointed, ahead and slightly to the right. "See that… over there?"

Bell strained forward in his saddle, peering. He said: "See something. Or think I can. Not sure." He rubbed at his smarting, aching eyes with the back of a gritty hand. "There's such a bleedin' shimmer!" he said.

The Sergeant turned in his saddle. He called to Pearson, now riding, with the officer's charger, as first file: "Pass the word for Brown."

"Brown!" went a shout. "Brown! Brown!" and the man cantered his horse presently up the line, past the walking horses of his fellows.

"Brown," said the Sergeant, "you've got eyesight: what d'you make that out to be?" He pointed again.

Brown dropped the reins on his horse's neck and fumbled, with both hands at the back of his head, to undo the tape which kept in position his sun-goggles of green talc. All had such goggles, but those who used them were evenly divided against those who did not. The goggles had advantages and disadvantages. Those who did not use them wore them, like two great staring eyes, up round their helmets over the pugaree.

The knot eased, Brown slipped the goggles from his eyes, which followed now the still pointing arm. He said:

"Trees. A clump of 'em. Absolutely."

"H'm." Bell shifted uneasily in his saddle. "Mirage."

"My foot!" said Brown. "Palms all right, Sergeant. 'Where beneath the golden palm, the silver water sings.'"

"Right. Thanks. Fall back." The Sergeant turned to his second in command. "He's right, Bell."

The Corporal blew out his lips. "Maybe. Or maybe not. He's mad, anyway. 'Artist' he calls himself."

"Good soldier, though," said the Sergeant.

"Mm! Certainly known worse."

They rode on in silence. Imperceptibly the Sergeant altered his course, so that now, instead of marching by the compass, he took that distant break in the desert's monotony as his guide.

Brown was right, for no mirage was this, but trees and water: a knoll of green in a waste of glaring, throbbing, dun and grey desolation.

But it took them five hours' march to reach it: six altogether, for at seven o'clock the Sergeant halted them, ordering all but two of the horses to be unsaddled. There was water, a little, and food of a sort for men and beasts. Food which could barely be swallowed for the torturing inadequacy of their drink.

For an hour the men lay about in the sand; they panted with the heat, and sweat rolled from them. Three, too, of the horses lay. Of speech there was barely any, for their fatigue was great and their thirst and discomfort exceeded it. There was no shelter and the sun beat at them.

Only Hale was talkative. "Wot's Mespot?" he asked of the sky. He lay on his back, legs and arms outspread, beneath his head a doubled-up canvas bucket. "Wot's

Mespot? 'Y a wide expanst of sweet damn all wiv' a river runnin' froo it! Hon all sides, wot did the soljers see? 'Y, sweet Fanny Adams! Rahver be in the New Cut meself." No one answered: no one laughed. He raised his head and surveyed those nearest to him. He said: "Pore little darlin's!" and subsided again and lay softly singing to himself:

> "Sta-ar of the Ever-nin'
> Bee-ootiful Ever-nin' Star-ah-ar;
> Sta-ar of the Ever-nin'
> A-shinin' on ther…"

He broke off suddenly as Sanders, who lay near him, got to his feet and walked away. With his eyes Hale followed. He called: "Oy! Oy! You, Sanders! Don't you like my dulket teenor?"

"'Tisn't y'r voice," Abelson spoke from behind his recumbent horse, "it's the naughty, naughty words that was coming! … You pie-faced sod!" He swerved suddenly round as he lay and clutched at Sanders' ankle as he walked by.

The man came down with a rush, face foremost. Abelson laughed; a barking sound.

"Chubbarow, Abie!" said Hale. "Leave the pore bleeder alone." He sat up. "Wot abaht some nicet roast pork?"

Abelson jumped to his feet and crossed to Hale with the quick neat steps of a boxer. Morelli, interested, stood up. Cook and MacKay rolled over to watch. In the background, Sanders raised himself slowly to his feet. His eyes, his nostrils, his mouth; all were full of sand. He stood, limply endeavouring to brush it away. He paid, apparently, no attention to the quarrel. But his eyes were wild.

Abelson stood over the Cockney. He said:

"I've had too many remarks from yeh! Get me? Stand up. Come on, stand up!"

Hale sat on. He cocked his head back and grinned up at the Jew. "Moses," he said, "wot d'yer tike *me* for? Yore a perfessional scrapper; I'm not. If you ever so much as *starts* to 'it me, *I'm* goin' to kick *you* right stryte w'ere it 'urts most." He held up a minatory hand. "I means it, Aaron. I do! Shape up ter me, me lad, an I'll qualify yer for the 'Arem stakes, an' bleedin' quick too!"

Abelson crouched; his mouth worked, but no sound came out of it. He seemed about to throw himself on the other.

The Sergeant's voice spoke from behind him. It said:

"Get saddled up. Quick! No hanging about. Abelson!"

"Sergeant?" The Jew turned slowly.

"Your turn to lead Mr. Hawkins' horse. Take over from Pearson. Looka live now, you men." He turned and walked away.

Abelson picked up his saddle. "—him!" he growled. "As for yeh, Hale, yeh slimy, ignorant choot; just wait! … No hawkers! no organs!"

IV

THEY rode on. The sun dropped low and lower, then suddenly went.

There was a moon. A silver sickle in the spangled velvet of the sky. It flooded the waste and these moving specks that toiled across the sand. It bathed the higher places in the desert's floor with silver, and cast gaunt, pitch-black shadows in depressions invisible by sunlight. It gave a lying promise of coolness, and a true, almost ecstatic, peace after the sun's ferocity.

"Why," asked Brown of the sky, "does the moon make quiet?"

"Make quiet!" Morelli said. "You're nutty! Isn't it always as quiet in this blasted place as Aberdeen on collection day? Quiet! Huh!"

Brown turned his head. "You poor —!" he said. "You wretched, half-sized, measle-brained little abortion! You sawn-off, chirpy, slab-sided dumble!"

Morelli laughed. "Go to it, you big stiff!"

"But can't you see," Brown said, "what I mean? The sun makes noise: not a noise like a drum, or you snoring, or a shell; but just one bloody great *blare*. Then the moon comes and the blare goes and there's a sort of immense quiet." He dropped his reins and stretched his aching muscles with outflung arms. "God!" he said, "I'd like to paint this… *if* I could. I'd…"

"What *I'd* like," Morelli said, "is a quart of bitter! Cold! So God-damn cold it made me scream when it hit my guts!"

"Stinking materialist!" Brown shook his great shoulders. "But I suppose you're right." He pointed ahead. "You can bust those guts with pawny soon, anyhow."

"Yep." Morelli nodded, for before them, at the head of a rise steady but so slight as to be almost imperceptible until after three-quarters of its length it suddenly sprang up, was the clump of palms. They looked, in their blackness against the silver of the sand, like a piece of painted scenery. And, thought Brown, very bad scenery too. They'd never believe you if you did that.

"Ah'm thinkin'," said MacKay, "'at yon's proveedential."

"Ar!" Cook solemnly gave agreement.

"What far d'ye make the deestance? A' these rookies 'ull be thinkin' they're juist atop o't. But they'll be wrong, *as* everr. Yon's three-four mile yet."

"Ar," said Cook.

The old soldier was right. Every next minute, it seemed, they could be there among those trees, seeking the cool water; and every next minute found the distance seemingly undiminished.

But arrive they did. The sergeant halted them perhaps half a mile from the knoll; sent the Corporal forward with Hale and MacKay.

They were back within fifteen minutes.

Bell was smiling. "O.K.," he said. "Lot o' trees. A spring... good. Plenty dates. And... queer... a mutti hut, empty!"

The sergeant raised his eyebrows. "A hut, eh? Any signs of occupation?"

"Nary sign."

"How old?"

Bell scratched his chin. "We-ell… difficult to say. Number o' years, *I* should guess. It's crumblin' a bit in parts."

"Um! …" said the Sergeant. He lifted his voice. "Get mounted."

They rode on then and up into a corner of Paradise. There were trees here; real trees which cast upon the ground at their feet a long lattice of black and silver, cool shade and cooler moonlight. Here, in a clearing round which the palms stood sentinel, was a spring from which water and water and more water endlessly, prodigally, bubbled. Here, by night, was a calmness and peace promising shelter and solace by day; here was bounty in the midst of desolation.

"Dis-mount!" said the Sergeant. "And keep those horses well away from the spring."

On foot, the men had difficulty in obeying this latter order, for the horses, scenting water, grew restless. The nervous bay mare which Pearson rode put a heavy hoof upon his foot: he squealed and loosed the bridle and sat heavily: the mare made straight for the spring. She cannoned into Abelson, struggling with his own gaunt grey and the charger. She knocked Morelli from his feet, though he kept his reins and his horse. She burst out, finally, from the group.

The sergeant sprang at her head, catching the off reins close to the bit. He checked and soothed her. Bell jerked Pearson to his feet. "Go an' get the damn' horse," he said. "*And* keep her. For the love o' God, wake up, man!"

26

Presently there was an order. Each man had taken from the neck of his horse the "bilt-up" rope; these had been joined and pegged firmly to the ground; the horses, free of saddle and bridle, were tied by their head-ropes to the line and shackled; the men, cursing, were rubbing them down. MacKay and Cook, at the Sergeant's orders, were filling canvas buckets at the spring and passing down the line... one and a half buckets to each horse. The Sergeant was invisible.

He was in the mud hut which hid, in the darkness, among the trees on that side of the little clearing remote from the line of horses. The hut was perhaps twelve feet long by nine broad. Its roof was, like the walls, of dried mud, which, unlike the walls, had been laid upon woven straw strengthened with sticks. Save for a hole in one corner of this roof and one in each of its walls, the little house was sound. The holes in the walls interested the Sergeant. He knew something of building with desert-sand and water, but never had he seen holes made in the side of a mutti structure without that structure collapsing. He could not see well, for the hut was dark and very dark, but he felt about the edges of the holes. His fingers found cane, strips of it. The holes then, though vilely irregular, were windows. He rubbed at his jaw reflectively for a moment; then turned on his heel and went out and across the clearing to the men and horses.

"All watered, Sergeant," said Bell. "All rubbed down. Feed?"

The Sergeant nodded. "Yes. A third of the spare nose-bagsful. Right away. When that's done, the men can finish."

"Right!" Bell turned away.

"And… Bell!" called the Sergeant.

"Yes?"

"Tell 'em they can kip down in the palace." He jerked his head in the direction of the hut. "Everybody except the guard." He looked at the watch on his wrist, lifting the projecting cover. "Hm. Nearly ten. Revelly five; that's seven hours… call it seven and a half… Take three men for guard: two and a half hours' reliefs."

"Who?" said Bell.

"Can't choose," the Sergeant said. "Fall 'em in, now; number 'em off, and take two, five, and eight. Put them on."

"Right." Bell turned away again. The Sergeant, as he too turned, heard his voice, "Fall in! come on, now. Drop all that!"

Numbers two, five and eight were Abelson, Cook and Pearson.

"Dis-miss!" said the Corporal.

The men in a mass, went for the spring. The Sergeant was there. He said, "Now, take it steady. Steady!"

Some did; some did not. There was, however, none among them really ill for lack of water, so that even the greedy did not suffer.

They lay about a while, satiate: they smoked and ate such dates as they could beat off the high branches by slinging ropes with weights such as mess-tins or stirrup-irons tied to them. Not a man touched biscuit or put knife to a tin of the bully beef.

The Sergeant sat alone, his back to a palm-trunk. He smoked a slow pipe to its end, knocked out the ash against his heel, and stood up.

"That'll do. All to kip now. In the hut. Bell!"

The Corporal came.

"Got the guard?"

"Yes—Abelson, Cook, Pearson. That order."

"Right. You get along and sleep." The Sergeant turned and walked towards the little line of horses; Abelson, the first relief, already by them. On the other side of the clearing, Bell, like a collie, was getting his flock into their pen. Over his arm each man carried the two blankets which, folded, go beneath every cavalryman's saddle; and, under that arm, his sword.

The Sergeant walked up and down the line of horses. He tested the firmness of the pegs which anchored the line to the ground and those which fixed the heel-ropes strapped to each rearhind. He felt at headstall and head-rope knots. He ran quick hands over each horse. He found a swollen hock and two backs with incipient soreness, one more tender than the other. He called, in a low voice:

"Abelson!"

The Jew came; his hands were deep in the pockets of his breeches; he lounged, his rifle, hung by its sling, banged against his shoulders as he walked. In the silver light, filtering interlaced with black through the palm fronds, his face showed patchy, its expression unreadable.

"Smarten up!" The Sergeant spoke sharply. "And carry that rifle. Don't sling it." He paused while the weapon was transferred from shoulder to hand. "This your horse?" he asked.

"Yes."

"Thought so. I've told you before. Look at his back. To-morrow you'll ride Mr. Hawkins's. See? And lead this. And be careful of your blankets. Don't *think* there's a space right through, make sure. Pull 'em well up under the front arch before you girth up."

"Right, Sergeant." Abelson was pleased: monotony broke him, and even the prospect of a change of horses, though a reflection upon his care, was a change, and therefore good.

"Tired?" the Sergeant asked.

The man nodded.

"Hm! Well, it's only about two hours. Got a watch?"

"Yes, Sergeant."

"Right, wake your own relief. Who is it? Cook or Pearson?"

"Cook."

"Right. And if you want me, I'll be sleepin' *outside* the hut. Where that bit of grass is at the back, the far side. Don't forget. 'Night." He walked to where his saddle lay, behind his horse, and took from on top of it his blankets. He bore these off into the darkness and pitched them in a heap at the foot of a tree behind the hut.

He set off then, through the trees, to the edge of the mound and climbed down it on to the level plain. He walked once round the knoll, his eyes searching the ground and the distance. He came up on to the knoll again as quietly as he might. He emerged from the trees at a point behind the line of horses, standing relaxed with hanging heads and limply straightened tails.

He left the shadow and stepped into a patch of silver light.

"*Whogerthere!*" Abelson stood in the dark shade of the next tree with levelled rifle.

"Friend." The Sergeant stepped nearer. "It's all right. Me."

"Christ!" The Jew laughed. "Thought you was a Buddoo, Sergeant. You nearly caught a packet."

"Quite right. 'Member where I'm sleeping if you want me. Tell Cook, and tell him to tell Pearson."

"Right, Sergeant. G'night, Sergeant."

"'Night." The Sergeant went again to where his blankets lay. He folded them each lengthways in four, then laid them down, horse-blanket first, one upon the other. He slipped off from his chest the ammunition-laden bandolier, and placed this, under the eight thicknesses of blankets, for a pillow. He took off his topee, dropped it by this couch, and lay down. His eyes, so heavy-lidded that for hours a conscious effort had been needed to keep them open, closed before his head was down.

The oasis slept. Every now and then would come a faint stirring as a horse changed its position, or the shuffle of a man's hushed footsteps as the guard walked up and down and roundabout. Between these sounds was silence; not the lesser noise that passes for silence in town or forest, but a lack of sound, utter and cruel and Absolute.

V

B Y stages at first imperceptible, then rapid, the moon lost its glory. It grew pale and lifeless and the last of its silver gave place to sickly pallor. The grey fingers of another day drove out gleam and shadows alike. The desert flattened again; dismally, terribly the same. A pale, dingy light spread itself, like the rays from a dusty lamp.

Then the sun came. Not gradually, but with a brusque suddenness like that of a conjuring trick. The dingy grey light was gone. The sun outrageously blared.

It mounted higher. A shaft came through the palms and struck the Sergeant's eyes as he lay. He waked.

He sat up, yawned once, and stretched himself. He glanced across the clearing, and, as if from a giant spring, shot suddenly to his feet. His right hand went to his breeches pocket and came away grasping the small, illegal automatic he had taken from the subaltern's pocket. In a jump he was at the hole in the hut's wall. He roared through it: "Turn out!" and raced away across the clearing.

There were no horses! Where the line had been was nothing; no beast, no rope, no peg. The saddles lay where they had, and across two of them was huddled the limp body of Pearson.

The Sergeant, after a darting glance this way and that which discovered nothing, knelt beside it. It lay face downwards the buttocks oddly thrust upward by reason of the saddle peak beneath the stomach. A dark pool, black against the light soil, was on the ground: drops to swell it dripped slow and thick from the saddle.

One hand beneath a knee, one beneath the head, the Sergeant picked it up and laid it down face upward, clear of the saddles. The eyes and mouth were staringly open: there was a great gash in the belly.

The men, rifles in hand, were round the Sergeant now as he knelt. They were silent; amazement held them. Many thought, just wakened from heavy sleep, that this waking was no waking at all, but dreams. They rubbed their eyes: they blinked: they shut their eyes and opened them again. They found they were indeed not sleeping.

"Bell!" said the Sergeant. He did not look round.

The men gazed at each other blankly. "Swelp me!" Hale said, and ran back across the clearing to the hut.

The Sergeant jumped to his feet and swung round.

"Bell!" he said. He scanned the faces. The body lay sprawled at his feet.

Abelson said, slowly: "Hale's gone for 'im."

All eyes went to the hut, saw Hale emerge, alone, and come racing towards them.

"Not there," he said, panting. "Nor his rifle neither. Or bandolier." He drew a deep breath. "There ain't nothink there, 'cept blankets an' the pack-saddle an' the omeyes an' the spare bandoliers."

The Sergeant said: "Spread out: make a circle round this place. Each man take about twelve yards. Push through the trees to the edge and *look*. Got me? Don't show yourselves. Look at the desert. Wait till I come round. And keep your eyes peeled. Get to it."

33

They went. Within a minute there was no sign of them nor sound. In the clearing the Sergeant stood. He looked down at the small, grotesquely sprawling body. He stooped and turned it on its face: the wound was not pleasant to the eye.

He straightened and stood looking about him. He discovered that sweat was pouring down his back, his legs, down from his head and over his face.

From the trees at the other side of the clearing came Brown. He waved urgently. The Sergeant ran to him. Brown seized his arm and drew him into the shade of the trees. After ten yards or so he stopped, pointing. "Alive," he said. "Just."

At the base of the palm, as if he were calmly sleeping, lay the Corporal.

The Sergeant found another knife-wound: in the back this time. The muscles, deep and broad and lithe, had saved the man from instantaneous death. He was breathing, but quick and light and weak, like a sickly child. As they gently lifted him, the wound opened wide and dark blood gushed.

"Careful!" said the Sergeant.

They carried him, half-upright, to the hut and made a soft bed with piled blankets, and upon it laid him face downward. Brown fetched water in a canvas bucket while the Sergeant, with careful knife, cut the shirt from the torso. They bathed the wound, which seemed clean, and the Sergeant drenched it with iodine from the little bottle in his field-dressing. But the cut, four inches long at least, gaped at them and welled blood as fast as they sponged.

"Wants a stitch," Brown said.

The Sergeant nodded. He found on the floor, in a corner Morelli's haversack and in it one of those cases called hussif. There were needles here and thick khaki thread. He took the finest of the needles, threaded it, and dipped all into the iodine. He knelt by the prone body and began.

Four stitches he made, neatly, in ten minutes. After that they strapped the wound with bandage from the field-dressing, over it strips of the torn shirt.

"That's about all we can do." The Sergeant got to his feet and stood looking down at the wounded man. "You stay here, Brown. Don't move him. But if he comes to, give him water… a little." He walked out of the hut and into the trees behind it.

He went cautiously, dropping to hands and knees as he neared the rim of the knoll. He found Morelli, lying flat, and lay beside him.

"Seen anything?" he asked.

Morelli cursed. He had, he said, seen nothing. There was, in his opinion, nothing to see, except sand. "And there's a helluva sight too much o' *that*!" he said.

The Sergeant's eyes too scanned the desert, and found nothing. He crawled fifteen yards and lay beside MacKay. Nothing. And so on round the circle of the knoll and the men who lay hidden in the fringe of tree-shade and coarse, rank grass growths. None had seen anything of life in the flaring sand which his gaze had raked. None had heard aught save his own movements.

Upright, the Sergeant walked back upon the tracks of his crawl. He sought MacKay.

He said, when he had found him:

"Jock, come down with me and walk round. They'll cover us."

"Ay!" MacKay got to his feet.

They slipped together down this, the steepest bank of their island, and cast the beginning of a wide circle about it.

They found, leading up to the knoll, the tracks the horses had made the night before as they arrived. They found, ten yards farther to the west, more tracks, leading away and out into the desert.

"Five abreast," said MacKay.

The Sergeant was silent for a moment. He said after a long pause: "That's that."

They completed their circle. They found… nothing.

VI

Save for MacKay and Cook, lying one at each end of the knoll, as sentries, the men were their own masters. The day had dragged; for, though there was water here, and shade, the heat was so little abated by these amenities that even untroubled idleness would have been a minor hell; and this idleness, enforced and full of meaning which none of them had yet dared openly to face, seemed intolerable.

They had, following the Sergeant's precept, bathed themselves and shaved. They had, since early morning and the discovery of their plight, taken in pairs the duties of look-out now filled by Cook and MacKay. They had, in turns, tiptoed into the hut to look at the Corporal, who, as yet, had neither stirred nor spoken nor opened his eyes throughout the dragging day while the Sergeant had sat beside him, watching and doing such little services as might be done. They had, many hours ago, carried the shrunken body of Pearson down into the desert and buried it deep. They sat, now, about the spring, their backs at trees, and waited for night.

"It beats hell!" Abelson said, breaking a silence. "How in the name o'—, the…"

"Shert up!" Hale looked up savagely from the pipe that he was scraping. "We've chewed the bleedin' rag abaht it all the bleedin' day. Wot bleedin' good's goin' ter come aht of any more bleedin' tittle-tattle? Chubbarow!"

"He's right," Brown said. "Let's chuck it. *Che sara sara.*"

Hale looked up. "Wot lingo's that?"

"Meant to be Italian."

"Macaroni, eh?" Hale put the pipe back into his pocket. "Bin there, Topper?"

Brown nodded. "Three or four times." His eyes wore now a lost, blank look of reminiscence.

The Cockney was persistent. "Wot's it like, eh? I've 'eard they lives on macaroni an' ving rooje exclusive. An' wot sorta place is there ere Veenis? Used to pump a lot o' yarn inter me when I was a nipper abaht it bein' a town in the water; goin' abaht in boats an' all that. Lot o' — tripe they do tell kids. Ever bin *there*, Topper?"

"Yes," said Brown, "It is in the water, sort of. And you do have boats instead of taxis. And it stinks: in the summer it stinks like hell."

"Worst o' them furriners: unclean lot!" Hale raised himself upright to spit.

"Yes. And no," Brown said. "But you forget the stink sometimes, or you get used to it, or it isn't there or something. And then it's marvellous. Bloody marvellous. They've got a moon there, a special one you can't see anywhere else. I'm not saying it's more beautiful than the one here—couldn't be—but it's... oh! absolutely different. It shines up from the water, too. Not from the surface, like ordinary reflections of ordinary moons, but right all the way up from the bottom... peering and staring and pushing great stabs of beauty up into your eyes..."

Hale reached out an arm and dug Morelli in the ribs. He nodded his head towards Brown, talking now as if to the palm fronds high above him. "'E's off!" he whispered. Morelli nodded.

"… so damn lovely it hurts," Brown's voice was saying. "And the gondolas have lanterns on them, swinging and dancing… coloured lights whose rays tickle the water … and then your gondolier… or someone's; anyone's… starts singing. And you lie there thinking you've never heard anything so wonderful… They all sing. Great, dark, creamy voices they've got…"

"'Ere!" Hale sat up. "'Ere! 'Ow the bleedin' 'ell *can* a voice be *dark*. I arst yer!" He sent an appealing glance round the circle.

"You shut y'r north, London," said Morelli. "You're an iggerunt bum. Show your manners an' don't cut in." He turned himself, still sitting, to face Brown. "Topper," he said, "what's the dick like out in Wopland?"

"That's it," Abelson agreed. "What about the skirt?"

"Ne' mind Levi!" Hale put in.

"I don't," Brown said. He sat silent a while, still with his eyes on the branches above him. Hale opened his mouth to speak, but Morelli thrust a quick elbow into his side, put a finger to his lips, and shook his head.

"Italian women," Brown said, "Italian women are fat and greasy and shapeless and smell of garlic and Italian women." He paused. "But Italian girls… an Italian girl can be the most lovely thing on this earth… Italian females should be poisoned at twenty-six. Before that age they should be honoured above all other women…

"There was a girl once," he said "… that was an amazing business… Lisabetta, they called her. My God! she was lovely…" He broke into laughter. "That *was* a funny show!"

"Well, corf it up, then," said Hale.

"You keep quiet." Morelli pulled him down and clapped a hand over his mouth.

"I'm not sure that it would *sound* so damn odd as it *was*," Brown said. He seemed to be talking more to himself than the others. "Venice, it was... about, um, seven years ago. There was a carnival... and Latin carnivals don't mean anything like fête-days at Hove or Battles of Flowers at Eastbourne, believe me... The whole town ... best part of it, anyhow... goes stark raving mad. I did ... and they last for days... You never know how long they last if you're in 'em, 'cos you get so be-yewtifully drunk... not a sleepy drunk or a vomiting drunk, but a splendid *mad* drunk; when you do damn silly things and they feel fine and look splendid; when all the colours in the world get together in your head and blaze in marvellous patterns; when you want to push houses over, and do; when you can fight like a mixture of Sam Langford, Hacken-schmidt and Cyrano de Bergerac, and make love like Juan...

"That time I'd been like that for... oh! a couple of days... I was sitting in some damn place... There was a hell of a crowd and flowers and that lead confetti you buzz out of cane-handled shovels... it stings like rain in hell... I was very, very drunk: I was sitting in a chair stuck on a table. They passed bottles up to me every now and then ... I had a damn great bag of that confetti and a shovel, and I was giving 'em hell as they came in... I remember, just before Lisabetta happened, there was a great fat Jew in a pink domino: I put three shovelfuls into his clock and he went out crying... And then I finished one of the bottles and I looked down... There she was! She had just a check domino over her ordinary clothes... and a dirty one at that. And her mask was off, hanging on one string from an ear whose tip you could just see under her black... blue-black hair. I yelled something, and was going to paste her with confetti... And then, though I was so very drunk... p'raps because I was... I saw that she wasn't in this game. That girl was frightened. Scared stiff as hell! She had great, enormous eyes... black, they were, and soft ... and a body that was a blessing. And her face was grey... these Latin women can't go white, but it's worse than white... and those eyes were terrified. Then they suddenly... cringed. A damn' great stiff, all togged up in a demon mask and red cloak came barging through the crowd and up to her: he caught hold of her wrist and said something, and she shook her head and tried to pull her arm away. Her lips were trembling and the grey-colour was lighter... Then... well, I dunno... I jumped off that chair and table straight on the big gink... he was about my size, but fat. He went buttocks over tip... I put my arm round the girl, and she leaned against me... I could feel her shaking... She said something; I couldn't catch the words, but I was on to it, all right...

"Fatty got up from where he'd gone and came at me ... He had his head down and his arms goin' like a round-about... I plonked him a snorter, and he changed his angle and lay down backwards and his nose fairly spouted from under the mask... *Then*, by God, *the* most amazing thing happened… This girl, this frightened kid, she just slid out from under my arm, and I looked, and there she was with a knife… Just as she was chucking herself on top of Fatty, I managed to grab her… She dropped the knife and threw a sort of faint…

"There was one great inferno of a row then. I had Lisabetta draped over one arm and Fatty got up and came at me again. I wasn't free to smash him, of course, I had to wait until he was close, and he got me a couple… on the top of the head, if you please. And he was holdin' his fists like hammers, soft part down… They didn't hurt. I poked him hard in the guts, and gave him a peach on the chin as he doubled up… He lay about then, underfoot, with every-body walkin' on him, his friends and all…

"The row went on… a hell of a row. Only Latins can make a row like that… There was a sort of boil in the café place, with me and Lisabetta the head, and round us the inflamed part… about twenty Italians yelling and wavin' their arms… and round them the ordinary healthy skin, the crowd who didn't know there was a row and went on drinking and yelling and singing and dancing and throw-ing confetti… All the twenty were screaming at me and each other and shaking dirty fingers under my nose and each other's… I believe some of 'em were on my side, but, dammit, you couldn't tell… I just stood there, with this girl still like a napkin over my arm and yelled at 'em. I said, 'Shut up, — you!' in every language I could think of… They didn't take any notice and suddenly, still bein' beautifully drunk, I saw a great deal of red…

"I put the girl over one shoulder, the left, and I went through that ring like a hot spade through a pound of butter... I don't suppose more than three of 'em went over really, but as I remember it, it seemed that the whole lot went flying this way and that... I went on and got into the rabble of people who had nothing to do with our little piece of bother... I wasn't thinkin' of that, of course; in fact, I don't know what I *was* thinkin' about... Anyhow, I started scrapping everybody, making for the door...

"Not having seen the row, they didn't like me a bit... Some of 'em, I expect, thought I was pinching the girl... They resented me... I got into a hell of a mess... Then Lisabetta came to or something; anyhow she slipped off my shoulder and stood by herself, and... just disappeared... I had to go on bein' militant, of course, 'cos everybody was very naturally hating my guts by this time... I collected several thick ears and a thump on the eye with a bottle... luckily it didn't break... and then I sort of felt that there'd be knives in a minute... There were. I saw one come out, then another... There was a chair... It had someone on it, very drunk, but I took it from under him... I wielded that chair, believe me... I was drunk, and fighting mad *and* scared... I didn't like knives...

"I got to the door... minus three-quarters of my clothes and a good deal of skin... but I got there. I remember looking back from the doorway... Dear God! that place *was* untidy... I was blowing like ten grampi, and I leaned against the wall. A hand... a soft, warm little hand... grabbed at my wrist. It was that girl. She kept talking... a stream of it.

My Italian, drunk, wasn't up to it. But she kept pulling and pulling, so I went… She began to run, so I ran… I found she was right, 'cos just as we turned a corner I saw that café absolutely spew out men… all after my blood!

"We ran like hares… We came out by one of the small canals… There was a gondola… She shot a spray of Italian at the gondolier, and we fell into that boat and crawled into the cabin-place and lay puffing on the cushions…

"As we drifted along we heard the chase go by… Phew! I was glad they wouldn't get me, I can tell you … Unpleasant noise they were making… She asked me, suddenly, for money. I had a lot on me… She gave the gondolier the whole fistful I'd taken out of my belt … then she came back to me again. I was sobered up a bit now, and I could get her Italian… 'I have told him,' she said, 'to go on. All night. All night. He will. There is a great deal of money now in his purse.' … He did. He went on…" Brown's voice tailed off into silence. He said, after a moment:

"That was *the* most wonderful night… It was as if the world was nothing… as if there wasn't a world… just a—a buoyancy on which one floated…" He laughed a little. "Or two, rather… I didn't see the water, or the sky… But I felt them… I can't explain… And we could, when our eyes got used to the darkness, see each other… just faintly…" He fell silent again.

A long pause was broken by Abelson.

"But what *about* it?" he said. "Did yeh…"

Hale shouted at him: "Fer God's sake shert up, Aaron. Ain't yer got *no* 'magination!" He turned his eyes on Brown. "But all ther sime, Topper, yer didn't ought to leave us 'igh *an'* dry like that?"

"They all," Morelli said, "wants licenshus detail. *You* know: what you'd call 'colour.' An' lots of it! You can't give 'em too much. Bibis, bibis an' more bibis."

Brown was filling his pipe. He said: "They're not goin' to get it. What their minds run to 'll be much more exciting than my shots at description… And anyway, I wouldn't tell 'em."

From behind the tree against which Brown leaned came Sanders. Now that he was clean and shaven the thinness of his face was startling, and from out of its even, dark-grey tan the pale blue eyes blazed with a disturbing intensity.

There came a moan from Abelson: "Here's old creeping Jesus! Where the — hell 'a *you* been, Soapy? At prayers?"

He was ignored. Sanders stood at Brown's feet and looked down at him. When he spoke his voice was taut and hard, and it trembled very, very slightly. His hands were clenched at his sides, at the end of rigid arms, so that the knuckles shone glaringly white against the bronze. His lean, narrow shoulders were hunched so that his chest was a hollow between them. He said:

"Brown! I want a word with you, Brown!"

"Speak on," Brown said from the ground lazily. His eyes were still misted with Venetian memories.

"I would rather…" Sanders hesitated. "I would, in a way, rather have spoken to you in private… But that were cowardly! I will say it here," he glanced round upon the others, his mouth curling, "before these… I will say it in spite of…"

Brown interrupted. He said: "For the Lord's sake, Sanders, don't be so intense. It's too hot."

Words came foaming from Sanders' mouth. "Is there any need," he cried, "for you to mock me before you've heard what I have to say to you? Listen to me, Brown! Listen! I have lain, there, behind that tree, all the while you have been talking. If it had been one of these others who had told these things, perhaps—weak fool that I am!—I should have risen and walked away, have suffered such foulnesses to go on. But it was you. Brown, who were talking. You! the only man in this small company from whom, as a man of gentle breeding, I…" He clapped, with a sudden, jerkingly mechanical movement, a hand to his forehead. "At times," he said, and his voice now shook uncontrolled, "I feel that I can't bear this longer… the foulness… the sordid retchings of base minds… the…"

Brown had wriggled until he sat upright, his great arms, naked from wrist to bicep, locked round his knees. He said, his deep lazy voice cutting across the trembling, whispered shout:

"What's all this *for*? If you don't like a cesspool, you're not forced to lie with your nose in it."

"What is it for? What is it for? You ask!" The shaking, precise voice rose to a thin but undisguised shout. "It is for you! For your sake, Brown! I implore you—think!

Is your life to be nothing but a foetid chapter of brawling and drunkenness and lust. Has it been nothing but this, that here, now, probably near to your death, there is nothing for you to do but live it all again in reminiscence, letting these other dogs nose your vomit with you?"

Brown let himself fall back on his elbow. "Oh, pack up!" he said wearily. "It's too hot to listen. And don't shout so." He rolled over and lay upon his stomach, tracing arabesques with his finger in the loose, sandy earth.

"But…" began Sanders on a high, cracking note.

"Close that belching trap of yours, J.C.!" Abelson followed his words with a clod of earth, which burst on the man's thin shoulders.

Brown sat up again. "You keep quiet yourself, you pox-ridden Jew!"

Abelson stiffened. "Whassat?"

"I said," Brown repeated, "'you pox-ridden Jew.' All right; all right. It's no damn' good… not a little bit… you gettin' your hackles up at me. I know you're a scrapper. I've seen you fight. You're good. But you strip at eleven-two. In shirt and trousers I go fourteen-ten, an' it's *not* fat, an' I *do* know a little about rough-housing. Get me?"

The Jew mumbled something in his throat and was quiet. Sanders was standing his ground. His fingers were working, coiling and uncoiling; his mouth, too, worked. There fell an uneasy silence.

"Brown," said Sanders at last: his voice was controlled now; low and urgent. "Brown, have you ever heard of Christ?"

"Christ? Oh, yes," Brown said. "Name's often mentioned." He lay once more upon his belly and was elaborating his design in the earth.

"Brown." said the low, almost choking voice. "He was the Son ot God."

"Not necessarily," said Brown. "Most improbable."

Sanders bent over him, shaking. "Do you add blasphemy to your list, then?"

Hale spoke in Morelli's ear. "'E's up it! Topper didn't oughter argue wiv 'im; 'e'll go pop in a minute. Pore sod! 'E always was queer. But 'e's bin gettin' queerer an' ruddy queerer…"

"Brown's right," Morelli muttered. "Do the guy more good to spew it up than keep it festerin' inside."

"Maybe!" Hale's tone was dubious. "Jus' 'ave a dekko at 'im!"

Sanders was bending over Brown, who still drew in the sand. Sanders' hands were fists, which made little awkward gestures in the air; his whole body looked as though it were set on an overpowered spring. He was saying: "But Brown … what, *what, what* is it that you… believe in?"

Brown left his drawing: he levered himself to his knees: he stood and leaned against the palm trunk, looking down at Sanders. He said:

"What do I believe in? … Oh, the taste and strength of wine: the loveliness of women: the feel of the sea when you swim in the Mediterranean: pints of beer in a country inn: the flapping of a sail: the weight of a fist: the colours of that ten-minute glory called sunset we shall see in an

48

hour: steak and kidney pudding: George Brown: a horse: a child's grin and a harlot's hiccup: Rugby football and the smell of a beech wood in autumn: the comfort of a woman's breasts and an old pair of shoes: strength: the asinine futility of this war: the splendid feeling of killing men: being frightened: being drunk enough to be brave: the smell of incense and the taste of bacon: toothache and triumph…"

"Stop!" Sanders' voice had gone back to its high, cracked shout, louder than before.

"All right," said Brown.

"Do you think it fine to mock me?" He took a step forward: his pale eyes blazed up at Brown's above them.

"I wasn't indulging in mockery," Brown said quietly. "If you keep a grip on yourself and try… just try… and see that there are other points of view…"

Sanders smote his forehead again, with that strange, jerking action. "Other points of view!" he cried. "You dare to talk of points of view…" He broke off, words tangling on his tongue. He made sounds in his throat, almost sobs.

"Sanders!" came the Sergeant's voice.

They turned. They had not heard him. He stood by the spring within six yards of them.

"Sanders!" he said again.

The man relaxed, the tautness went from him. He turned and walked towards the Sergeant, his gait unsteady. "Yes?" he said.

The Sergeant was intent upon the unravelling of a knot in the lanyard which ran from his belt to his hip-pocket. He said, without looking up:

"Just go in and sit with Corporal Bell, will you? If he moves or anything, let me know."

Sanders went. The Sergeant's eyes, no longer on the knotted cord, followed him until he disappeared into the hut.

The Sergeant walked over to the group. "I want," he said, "to talk to you men." Hale and Morelli showed signs of getting to their feet. "No, sit down," he said. Brown, tired of standing, took this order literally. The Sergeant leaned a shoulder against the same palm and looked down at them. He said, after a pause:

"What d'you think of the position we're in?" He turned his head to look directly at Brown.

"Sticky," said Brown. "Damn' sticky."

The Sergeant looked at Morelli.

"Dunno at all," Morelli said. "Can't make head nor tail of it."

"We're done," said Abelson. "That's what *I* think. Bitched!"

The Sergeant's glance rested on Hale, who said:

"Much as I regrets it, Sergeant, yours truly's compelled to agree wiv Moses 'ere! We are!"

"I'll tell you," the Sergeant said, "what I know."

VII

T HEY waited in a long silence before he spoke.

"I know," he said, "nothing. I'll be open with you. I don't know where we are. I don't know where we were goin'. I don't know where the Brigade is, I don't know which way they were goin' to move. I've got compass and map. But, as you'll 've seen, these don't help; not in the circumstances."

"We are…" began Brown.

"What I said," finished Abelson. He laughed, bewildered, and his red lips curled back from the over-white teeth. "And—! *And*—!"

"We are," said the Sergeant. "If we say so. The horses 've been pinched. That's Arabs. No one else on earth could 've got 'em away like that and not waked a soul. So we're up against hostile Buddoos. Not Turkish Army. At present there aren't many of 'em…"

"How not?" said Abelson.

Brown glanced at him. "Because, you bloodstained Pilate, if there'd been more than a few they'd 've had at us. *And* wiped us out."

The Sergeant nodded. "Exactly."

"Spoken to Jock, Sergeant?" Morelli asked.

"I have. He agrees with me that there can only be a few. He says not more than three. It's my theory that however many of 'em there were 've gone off, with our goras, to their pals. They may all come back… or not."

"Ten to one… fifty to one… they will," said Brown.

"If nothing prevents 'em; yes. But somethin' might. They may be a wanderin' lot."

51

"They'll come!" Abelson smiled again. "They'll come!"

Hale turned on him. "Fer Christ's sake give over! Yore a bloody chorust of bleedin' woe!"

The Sergeant said: "Well, I've told you. Better for us all to know." He took his shoulder from the tree trunk and stood upright.

"But what the hell," put in Abelson, "are we going to *do*?"

"We stay," said the Sergeant, "where we are. Abelson, I've been hearing you blinding and cursing about too much sun and not enough pawny and all that. You ought to be happy." He looked down into the Jew's upturned eyes. "An' you'd better *be* happy. See?" He paused a moment; then took them all into his glance again. "We've got to *see*," he said. "We've got to see for miles. Observation post wanted. It's no good from practically on the level as we are here. You think you can see everything on a desert. But you can't. Hardly anything. When we can see we can signal. Or not, accordin'. Anyway, we'll *know*."

"We can't slog it on foot somewhere?" Brown looked up with creased forehead.

"It's nearly, so far as one can make it without knowing our exact position, nearly seventy miles to the nearest point of the river. Couldn't carry the water," the Sergeant said. "Or Bell," he added.

Brown shrugged. "I got you, Sergeant." He looked up at the great straight trees above him. "You could see a bit from up there." He pointed to the still, sharp fronds that looked so stiffly artificial.

"Exactly," said the Sergeant. "Look-outs there all day, in reliefs of one. Three sentries, in reliefs of three, all night. And we start now. Morelli!"

"Sergeant?"

"They left us the saddlery. Bring all the reins. Right away."

"I'm the Hawk's Eye, Sergeant. Me first?" Brown rose and stretched himself, flinging out his great arms.

"Right," said the Sergeant.

"But I'm no gory albatross," Brown muttered. "Ain't got no wings, brudder." He cast his eye up the rough, bare trunks, branchless for twenty feet or more.

The Sergeant heard him. "Morelli's bringin' you a tail."

He took the great bunch of leather strips. "Start in knottin' 'em," he said. "Better use bowlines. Who knows knots?"

"Me." Brown sat and began weaving the leather.

"And me." Morelli followed suit.

There was thus in a few moments a leathern rope of sixty feet or more. "Four or five stirrup-irons," said the Sergeant. They came and he tied them, in a bunch, to one end of the line of leather.

"Casters ahoy!" Brown bellowed, and leapt to his feet. "That's me too, Sarge." He took the line. "Stand clear!" he roared. The bunch of steel whistled, in an ellipse growing wider and wider as he paid out the slack, obliquely round his head, soaring above it to one side and almost touching earth at the other.

"Weeeee!" said Hale, as the weighted line, released, sailed up in a soaring sweep. "Oh, Gawd rot my boots!"

The irons had fouled some fronds, hung a moment and come crashing down.

There were three more false casts, two by Brown and one by Abelson.

"You bastard!" Brown said to the leather. He took it again. He swung, for minute upon minute. He let go. The irons sailed, their brown tail behind them. They flew straight, clearly over the branch and down to earth again.

"C'est magnifique, ça!" Brown bowed to his audience. "Verree deeficult, that treek! Right away, Sarge!"

The Sergeant smiled. "Yes. Quicker the better."

"Ach! Zo!" Brown capered; he rubbed his feet in imaginary resin, his hands on an imaginary handkerchief thrown by invisible assistants. He cocked his topee over one eye and minced up to the tree. Hale let out his shrill cackle of a laugh. Morelli clapped. Abelson made noises as of a roll on the drum.

Brown seized the double line and shook it. "Zilence!" he roared. "Zilence of the mosd abzolute there musd be while ze Brofessor his mosd marvelloz veeds do berform!"

He began to climb. By reason of the thickness of his boots and the thinness of the reins, he could not give himself aid either by clipping the line with his feet or "walking" the trunk. He climbed solely by the power of his arms.

"Gosh!" said Morelli. "That's over fourteen stone he's hoistin'. Strong as an ox!"

"Yup." Hale nodded.

They watched while slowly but with seemingly perfect ease he finished his climb and got both hands on to the angle made with the trunk by the slender branch which seemed so inadequate for his weight. He looked down at them. He shouted:

"Heya! Heya! Is it da man or da monk? Applouse, pleez!" He pulled himself up and wedged one knee into the crook and put weight upon the trunk with his hands. "Veree, veree, deeficult!" he called. "Mos' dangereuse. Ziz brave man play wiz Death for your entertainings!"

He gradually stood. He could reach other branches. He began to climb and presently found a comfortable crook and settled himself into it.

"They're fraygile, them things," muttered Hale. "'ll they bear 'im?"

"They're tough as hell," Morelli said.

The Sergeant withdrew his eyes from Brown in the tree-top. "Get these spare reins gathered up," he said. "And you an' Morelli, Hale, will relieve Cook and MacKay. Right away. There's only about an hour to sundown, and the night guard 'll be a different arrangement."

A shout came from above. They looked up. They could see, though Brown was motionless, that an excitement had seized him.

"Hi!" He looked down for an instant and called out something their ears could not catch.

"Whassat?" cried the Sergeant, hands cupping his mouth. Hale and Morelli, beside him, craned their necks.

There came then two sounds, so nearly together that never could they tell, though all heard both, which had first come to their ears... A faint and distant "phut"... a near and appalling crackling and crashing...

"Stand clear!" bellowed the Sergeant. He thrust Hale to the left, Morelli to the right. He leapt backwards.

There was a dark rushing, ending in a thump which seemed to make the ground shake beneath their feet.

It was Abelson, farthest away, who first acted. He ran to the body and knelt beside it. He lifted the head, its topee gone. There was a neat round hole in the forehead, two inches above the left eyebrow. The edges of this hole were faintly discoloured with blood.

The Jew lifted the head farther and crouched to peer at the back of the skull. There was another hole. He lowered the still head and limp great shoulders gently to the ground.

"My... *God!*" breathed Morelli. Hale made little whistles through clenched teeth.

The Sergeant, with a suddenness almost alarming, leaped over the huddled body and ran in three strides to the tree and seized the double leather line. He put his weight upon it and began to climb. He was barely off the ground when the line, with a crackling of torn and damaged wood, came down with a rush. He staggered back and fell.

Morelli, paralysis over, ran back to where they had sat by the spring. From where it leaned against a palm he snatched his rifle. He began running towards the western fringe of the knoll.

"Stand clear!" bellowed the Sergeant.

The Sergeant picked himself up. "Morelli!" he shouted. Morelli halted in his tracks, impatiently turning his head. "Come back!" The Sergeant made emphatic gestures. Morelli hesitated; then ran on. The Sergeant put hands to his mouth, "*Morelli!*" There was something in that shout that halted the runner: he stopped, hesitated, and turned. He came slowly back, with dragging steps. His head was bent. He dragged his rifle, the butt making in the sandy soil a groove which trailed behind him like a snake.

"Hale," said the Sergeant. "Abelson. Get your rifles. Quick!" They ran, and returned. The Sergeant bent down and peered at the limp mass which had been Brown. He said:

"That shot came from somewhere that side." He pointed west. "He was facin' that way. It was a long shot. Very. Hale, go out to that side about quarter-way between Cook and MacKay. Don't show yourself. Make one great eye of yourself. Get! … Morelli, do the same, about half-way between Hale and MacKay… Abelson, go along to MacKay and find out whether he's seen anything. Then the same with Cook. Jildi!"

He watched them go; then turned and ran across the clearing. At the doorway of the hut he stopped and called softly: "Sanders!"

Sanders came, blinking at the light. "The Corporal," he said, "hasn't…"

"That'll do." The Sergeant was brusque. "Make a back. I want to get on top here." He pointed at the hut's roof.

"I don't under…" Sanders began.

"Come *on*!" said the Sergeant. "Make a back! Put your hands *there*... and bend a bit. I want to get on the roof."

He got there presently. Below, Sanders rubbed at his bony shoulders. The Sergeant, standing delicately at a corner of the flat roof where the thick wall joined it and gave support, shaded his eyes with one hand from the slanting rays of the dipping sun. He peered westward. As he had imagined, he was high enough here to see out, between the palm trunks, over the desert; but not so high that the palm fronds obstructed his view.

His eyes searched the waste. They saw sand and sand and sand. A few dips and ridges like low, quiet waves. But nothing more... No life... Nor, it seemed, anything ... any hole or crack or mound in, behind, or about which men could hide.

But Brown had been shot... That was that... So, somewhere within range, there was... someone. He strained his eyes until black specks floated before and round him in the hot, still, lifeless air.

He cursed beneath his breath. He gingerly crouched and sat, and finally slid from the roof. He landed in a heap; to find Sanders standing over him. He got to his feet. "Better get inside again," he said. "How is he?" He jerked his head towards the wall upon the other side of which lay Bell.

"He seems stronger." Sanders spoke hesitantly. "His breathing is not so light and quick as it was." He paused; turned away; halted and turned again. "Sergeant!" His voice was urgent, already reaching for its higher note. "Sergeant! what was... what has happened?"

The Sergeant looked at him. He said, slowly and quietly, watching the thin, drawn face:

"Brown's been killed. He was up that palm... somebody shot him. He was dead at once."

Sanders drew in his breath with a sharp hiss. He stood silent, with bent head. His lips moved rapidly. The Sergeant glanced at him, then turned away. "Get back inside," he said.

VIII

THEY buried Brown after sunset, down on the desert to the east side of the oasis. Three carried his body, Morelli and Hale and Cook. On that side of the knoll, above them, lay Abelson and MacKay: rifles rested before them, they watched. On the other fringe, looking out to the west, were the Sergeant and Sanders. No sound nor sight disturbed the work.

They gathered, afterwards, about the Sergeant, who stood now by the spring. He chose a night-guard; three three-hour reliefs of two men each. First, Hale and Abelson; second, MacKay and Cook; third, himself and Morelli. Sanders, offered change from his nursing duty, shook his head. No; he would continue; he could snatch, he thought, a few minutes' sleep here and there.

They had a meal of sorts doled out by the Sergeant; to each a hard biscuit, the seventh part of a tin of bully beef, dates. They sorted themselves for this meal: Hale and Abelson and Sanders ate theirs at their posts; MacKay, at the Sergeant's order, sat with him over by the hut, leaving Morelli and Cook by the spring.

Inside the hut, Sanders devoured his food: he ate with a speed which did not arise from hunger but rather from a desire to be done, as quickly as might be possible, with a tiresome and unpleasant but necessary operation. The last crumb barely swallowed he knelt beside the sprawling, immobile body of the Corporal. He cast back his head: his face, the eyes closed, wore a look enrapt. The lines went from it; it became smooth and calm, but yet, somehow, the face of a man in pain. His lips moved, soundlessly, and his hands were clasped, high before his chest, with such force that the knuckles shone white.

By the spring, Cook ate with slow enjoyment. He cut his little square of beef into small cubes, each of which he set upon a larger section of his carefully-broken biscuit. He chewed deliberately at each mouthful, and between mouthfuls took draughts of water. Morelli watched, his own food untouched before him, resting on the side of his flat-lying water-bottle. He said, suddenly, the first words that either had spoken:

"Like this? I don't want it." He held out his biscuit and meat.

"Ar!" said Cook. He put out a hand, enormous, and received the food. He nodded by way of thanks.

Morelli was restless. He sat; he stood; he walked about in narrow circles and sat again. He repeatedly brought out, jerkily, words meant as the beginnings of remarks he did not make. He pulled out his pipe but found no tobacco; put then a cigarette between his lips; changed his mind and thrust it back into his leather case. He stood, now, looking down at the other, who still stolidly chewed. He said:

"Cookie! You ever get… upset like… 'bout anythin'?"

Cook, drinking, shook his head slowly from side to side. Morelli sat, abruptly and with a sort of finality in his action as if he were determined, now, that this should remain his position. He looked down between his hunched-up knees.

"Not never?" he said. "S'pose they was to get Jock… next? What 'bout *that*?"

Cook withdrew from his mouth the finger which had been pursuing a clinging string of the bully beef. He pondered, looking at this finger blankly.

"Ar!" he said at last.

Morelli seized on the inflection. "There!" he said, "that shook you! Well... that's how I'm feelin'... You was a sailor, Cookie? ... You know about them guys they call ... what is it? ... Jonahs?"

Cook nodded decisively. "Ar." He had finished his meal now. He drew his legs up under him, crossing them and wedging the ankles beneath his solid thighs. He groped in a breeches pocket. His hand came away with a cake of black tobacco. He bit off this cake a lump. His jaws began to work with a steady rhythm. Save for their movement he was motionless as the palms behind and before him. Now the moon was flooding the clearing with soft silver light, and Cook, half-bathed in this light and half in black shadow, was like a stone Buddha, square, thick; immobile and immutable.

"... Jonahs!" Morelli was saying. "Guys what bring bad luck... I'm one o' them, Cookie... I'm a Jonah... I am, sure! To me frien's, anyways." He stopped, his voice dying away; tailing off, as it were, into the light and darkness and silence.

Cook chewed. Every now and then, his only movement, his head would turn as he shot from his mouth a dark jet of saliva and tobacco juice.

"A God-damned bahstud of a Jonah... that's me," Morelli said. "... To me frien's... I've always been noticin' it, ever since I was *so* high… Whoever gets tangled up with me… friendly-like… so he, *or* she, gets it right slick where the chicken got the axe… Started when I was at school, it did… That's funny, too, now I think… there was a kid called Brown… he was a sidekicker o' mine: got a public birchin' through me… Now there's old Brownie… not that his coppin' that packet was *through* me, exact … but we *was* half-sections *and* he's got his… Good guy, old Topper! Eh, Cookie?"

Cook spat again. "Ar!" he said.

"One o' the best!" Morelli unclasped the hands that locked his knees; he stretched his legs and lay back, crossed hands supporting his head. He went on, his voice very low. "Why the — *hell*," he said savagely, "should *he* click before a — like that choot of a Jew-boy, or that tin-faced Bible thrasher? Or me? … No reason! No reason a-tall… But he was my half-section… Get that, Cookie? … How'd *you* like it, bein' a Jonah?"

Cook spat. He shook his great head, slowly, from side to side.

"'Course you wouldn't. Nobody wouldn't! And, by Mary, *I* don't! … I'm just an ornery little —! I don't *mean* any harm even if I don't mean much good… But it's just that way with me… Always the same… wi' women too… Take that turn o' mine, 'fore the war… That was as good a little team o' two as ever you saw, Cookie… Morel and Moree… that was us… *And* we'd of got somewhere, *if* I hadn't had this ju-ju Jonah business on me… We would that, believe *me*… Why in Chicago, though we was the first turn... y'know what *that* means... they gave us a coupla 'cores the very first night... When we left to go on to th' next o' the circle... Pittsburg... we was half-way up the bills, *and* in letters 'bout three-four inches high... Morel an' Moree: Specialty Dancers... Morel was me, see? An' Moree was Joey, bless 'er! ... That was a good kid, Cookie... There was some that said she was chee-chee... But that was all wind! ... She thought her gran was a Chink... that's all. And what if she was! Eh? ... Joey was all right all right! And *dance*! She was a looker, too... p'r'aps there was some who wouldn't of said that the first time they saw 'er. But she grew on you, did Joey... We wasn't married, Cookie, but if ever a little sawn-off runt of a 'centric dancer got a wife a helluva sight too good for 'im, that was me after I found Joey."... His voice died away again, he lay on his back, his eyes blankly staring up through the tracery of the palm leaves at the star-blazing sky.

Cook was still and soundless and... permanent. Morelli did not look at him. He started to talk again, his voice so soft that it seemed a part of the breathless night.

"... We was pretty damn' happy, Morel an' Moree! ... I should *say*! ... Happy as... whatever's happy... All the time, we was... and then, out in the States, with the turn goin' so good 'n everything... well, there wasn't no holdin' us, believe me! ... We was knocking down good money, too...

"But I'm a Jonah... I've told yer... a bleedin' ugly great sod of a Jonah... What happens? ... Why, our second time in Chicago there's a feller sees Joey... he comes again… takes a front rower every night fer a week… Well, this guy, he's not one o' the lads after his greens, see? He's an Agent… name o' Mount… a guy that fixes up Managers wi' talent an' Arteests wi' jobs, see? … Well, this Mount, he sizes Joey up an' reckons she's the goods… reckons he could fix her with a two-year Noo York contract at God-knows-how-many bucks a week… an' all this just to *start* with… But he's fly, is Mount… He makes a few inquiries 'bout Joey an' me, an' he finds, roughly like, how things are with us… So he gets at Joey private… He doesn't write, see? He gets her one day when I'm out; an' he puts it to her in words an' gives her a letter on top o' that with it all down in black an' white, *and* red… 'Course, *I* never heard any o' this till after, becos… what d'you think that kid does… She tells Mount she'll think it over, an' she does think it over… *And* she decides that *I* wouldn't like it, as there wasn't nothing for me in it… So she writes this Mount a letter turnin' 'im down… all on her own an' never tellin' me damn-all…

"Then we goes on, for the second time, to Pittsburg… we're known there then an' we goes with a bleedin' zip an' zowie 'n everything, I can tell *you*… God! we were all right all right… then. Happy! I should *say*! …

"But I'm a Jonah, Cookie… *as* I've said… The third day in Pittsburg, Joey's out shoppin'… There's a coat she wanted… She'd made up her little mind to *have* that coat … She borrows a hundred bucks off me an' goes out laughin' all over her face… I was still lyin' in her bed… no revelly in those days…

"Cookie! she never came back to that room... God Almighty! I'm a Jonah, I tell yer! ... She was crossin' the road... *to* that shop, that *bleeding* shop... She's just stepped off the sidewalk when... *blim!* ... a damn lout drives his car right into her..."

Morelli sat up. His voice was shaking. He swallowed hard and cleared his throat. He put his empty pipe into his mouth and spoke with his teeth clenched round its stem.

"She wasn't killed... because I'm a Jonah... She wasn't killed... no such luck... No, sir! That smash does somethin' to her back... jiggers up 'er spine, somehow... An'... an' there she is, when I'm allowed to see her, 'bout two-three days after... lyin' flat in a nursin'-home bed... Flat, Cookie... flat as flat... An' white's a lot of linen... But she smiles at me... the same smile... an' she jest guys me a bit... *Some* kid, Joey! ... I should *say!* ..." He got to his feet and walked up and down, three or four steps in each direction, in front of the silent Cook.

"She's... still there, Cookie," he said. "Still there... in that same bed... so far's I know... had a letter from her last mail we had, at Sheikh Amid... Fourteenth o' March, '14, it was... when she got run down... An' there she is ... for keeps... It was her made me... well, not *made* me ... it was her who saw as I was thinkin' after the war started, that p'r'aps I oughta if it wasn't fer her... oughta come back an' join up... She made me leave 'er, Cookie...

"See what I mean... about this Jonah business?" He stopped in walk and looked down at the other. "See what I mean, Cookie? ... There was that Mount an' her contract… 'F it hadn't been for *me* she'd a' taken that… never 've gone that second time to Pittsburg… See, Cookie?"

"Ar," said Cook. He got to his feet. He began to walk. Morelli fell into step at his side. They walked, in silence, round the clearing, and round it, and round it.

"You're right," Morelli said, after the third circuit. "Exercise."

"Ar!" said Cook.

They saw, as they walked, the red, leaping glow of a small fire behind and to the left of the hut.

Beside the fire squatted MacKay and the Sergeant. MacKay held over the fire the lower half of a mess-tin, three-quarters full of a brownish liquid in which floated long string-like shreds. He stirred this liquid from time to time with a sliver of wood. He lifted the tin from the fire and peered into it.

"What's it like?" asked the Sergeant.

MacKay pulled a wry mouth. "We-el, it's no' *dainty*… Nor would Ah care t' be suppin' it mesel', if ye follow me."

"It's the best we can manage," the Sergeant said. "P'r'aps when we've strained the grease off, it'll do. It's got to."

"Ay! But when'll yon puir son-of-a-bitch ha' life in 'im to tek it? Answer me that."

The Sergeant rose. "Not so long. He's better, Jock. When I went in just now he was movin'… a little. And Sanders there, prayin' like an abbey full of monks."

"Yon'd pray th' feet off a comp'ny o' the H.L.I.!" said MacKay. "In ma opeenion yon Sanders' sire was a cab-horrse, and his dam had nine row o' brass dugs." He spat, tasted the brew, spat again and was silent.

"Bad as that, is it?" The Sergeant stretched out a hand for the mess-tin.

"No' quite," said MacKay. "But, d'ye know, in nigh on thairty year o' soldierin', Ah never tasted bully-broth afore." He passed the tin.

"It's all we can do. And that's that." The Sergeant sipped. "I dunno. It might be worse." He raised his voice. "Sanders!" he called softly.

Sanders came. His face was pale beneath its tan, and lines were graven deep upon it. But his eyes were almost peaceful; their flare had gone. "You called me?" he asked.

The Sergeant nodded. "How's he now?"

"The same, Sergeant. There has been no change at all since you saw him. He's still a little restless. And once or twice he has spoken; incoherently."

"Hm." The Sergeant scratched his head. "We'll leave him to-night." He held out the mess-tin. "Take that, Sanders. Keep it covered up. That's for Corporal Bell… when we can feed him. In the morning, start straining it… somehow… to get that fat off as much as you can." He watched while Sanders, mess-tin in hand, walked with slow, careful steps back to the hut and disappeared within it.

"Looks better, doesn't he?" The Sergeant turned to face MacKay again.

"Sanders? … Wee-ell…" The Scot was doubtful. "Mebbe yes; mebbe no… He sairtenly's quieter… But whot's that?

Mebbe only the calm afore the storm… Yon felley's goin'… mark me words!" He tapped his forehead.

The Sergeant changed the subject. "I'm going to tell 'em, Jock… To-night."

"Tell whot?"

"What I said to you after our talk just now."

"Oh… ay!"

"Weigh up the position… and be frank about it… Tell 'em our suggestion about the river… and ask 'em to draw for it…"

MacKay looked up. "Draw forr ut?" he repeated.

"Yes… Draw for it… Every one except Sanders. He'd be no more good 'n a wet Sunday… Just one draw. Whoever gets it picks his half-section…"

"But there's no' any need fer *drawin'*." MacKay was vehement. "Did not Ah say—"

The Sergeant cut him short. "You *said* all right. But what you say isn't necessarily what *I* do… No, Jock, every one's to be in this… it's a poorish business to send a man on, and we've all got to take a chance." He looked at his watch. "I'll do it when the first relief comes off… You must put it up to Cook, when you both go on… or just before… Better find him now; there's about half an hour."

MacKay went grumbling. The Sergeant was left squatting by the little fire. Its dying embers blazed angrily as he stirred them. A little spurting flame threw light upon his face as he crouched, casting into relief the rather high cheekbones and taut cheeks beneath them; the strongly-muscled jaw and deep-set eyes, wide apart, on either side the arrogant nose.

These eyes were bent upon the fire, unseeing. His lips moved, in prayer or curse. From behind him came a low crisp crack as Abelson, on his beat, trod upon and broke some fallen palm-leaf, thick and sinewy and brittle.

The Sergeant started. He found himself standing upright, the stick with which he had been stirring the fire fallen from his fingers. He became aware that every muscle in his body was rigid; that sweat had broken out upon his forehead… not such sweat as was habitual throughout these desert days and nights… but a sudden, cold douche of sweat. He turned to see the dim, shadowed figure of the sentry disappear among the trees.

He laughed at himself… a mirthless sound. He wiped his forehead upon his forearm; and his mouth curled.

"Jumpy!" he muttered, and went in search of his garrison.

IX

THE relief had changed. Cook and MacKay were now on duty. By the spring the Sergeant sat with his back at a tree trunk: facing him, sitting, lying, sprawling, were Hale and Morelli and Abelson. The moon was high now, over a man's head if he looked directly up, so that the clearing was a silver dish bounded by ebony and silvery tracery. Where they sat the light was strong; so strong that one could with care have read small print. The Sergeant had been talking. He had finished now, and there was silence.

The men were all without their helmets. The soft yet metallic light showed each the faces of his companions; showed them clear and yet strange, softening lines to which they were used, intensifying hollows and aspects never before noticed.

They were set, these faces, into a look of rather bewildered gravity. Smiles there were none; nor even… yet… the grins of desperation.

Hale spoke first, rolling from his side to his belly the better to look up at the Sergeant. He said:

"You says, Sawgint, as 'ow you want suggestions… But — me 'f there's anythin' to suggest. You've tole us… 'Ere we are… Ruddy well stuck! Well, wiv all joo respeck, we knew that afore…" He looked at Abelson and Morelli as if for confirmation. They nodded. "So what you've jus' tole us… that goes… An' 'ere's one as is ready for that draw now." He put his head down on his crossed arms.

"I agree," Morelli said. "Yours is the only way, Sarge… We gotta *try* somep'n… So let's get at it."

There was silence then. The Sergeant broke it. "Abelson?" he asked.

The Jew sat with his knees drawn up under his chin. "I s'pose it's right..." he said at last. "But *I* think the two of us that draws that job might 's well blow their — brains out as a start..."

"Hardly that," the Sergeant said. "It's a chance... p'r'aps a long one. But it *is* a chance..."

"H'm! ..." Abelson grunted doubtfully. "But the way I see it... look here... suppose ye're right about where we were an' the distance to the river... I say: suppose ye're right... and suppose whoever goes *does* get through... well, when they're there, what? ... We ain't a — pack of brass hats... Why the bleeding hell should there be any-one there... English, I mean? ... *we* don't know... They might be Johnny they found, see? Mightn't they... Or Arab choots... Or they mightn't be no one, not at all; and *then* what? Eh? ..."

"It's all guess-work, Abelson." The Sergeant spoke curtly. "It's got to be. It's doin' something based on proba-bilities. And that's all we've got to go on. D'you want us to stay here and rot... or get shot like a lot of piards? What else can we do? I've told you all I know and what I suggest. I needn't 've done that... but I have, 'cos we're in this, all of us, and we've got to get out. I asked for suggestions... and I'd be willing to consider 'em... but I didn't ask for moans... And I'm not goin' to have 'em... Now: have you got anything to suggest?"

Abelson glowered down at his knees. He said, hesitantly and almost in a mutter: "What about these soors been pooping off at us? Why not have a slap at 'em... Said yerself couldn't be many of 'em..."

"Right," said the Sergeant quickly. "Nothing we'd like better... How'll we start?"

Abelson was silent.

"Come on then. Tell us... How'll we start?"

"That's for you to say," Abelson mumbled.

"Is it? Well, I don't know how." The Sergeant had raised his voice a little now. It was clear and hard: it seemed to be making jagged little holes in the heavy moon-drenched air. "D'you think I've not thought o' that? D'you think so? With Bell there... and Pearson and Brown *there*! You say there's only a few of... whatever they are... You're right. There can't be many or they'd come up and attack us and mop us up... and p'r'aps that'd be a good job...

"No... there aren't many... Maybe only two... even one... But where are they? ... Say those that took the goras 've gone, which is probable... But they've left some... or *someone*... And now you're talkin', where is he or they? They've *been* within rifle shot... but are they still? ... D'you want the job of runnin' out to catch 'em... when you don't know where they are... over land with as much cover as a skatin' rink... Yes, I know you're goin' to say they're in cover. So they must be; but where's ours while we're lookin' for 'em? ... *They're* in some little nullah we can't see... over there..." He swung out his arm to the westward. "Y'know what the desert's like. You think it's all flat when you look… but oh, no, it isn't! … But there's one thing more: 'f we go lookin' for 'em, that's what they want… How many of us 'd get there? … And now you're going to say… so I'll say it for you… how about the two that go on this chance? Won't they get spotted and done in? I say they may… *that* we can't tell… but they won't by our pals that 've been payin' *us* attention. *They're* over there." He pointed again. "Whoever goes from here's got to go *that* way; the other way… Our pals haven't changed their hole, else the guard… we've had one on all the time… 'd 've been bound to see 'em… When the two go, the others 'll line that western side and watch…

"No, Abelson," he said, speaking more slowly now. "You've suggested nothing. The draw holds… We'll do it to-morrow and that night… p'r'aps the next… who gets it'll go."

"An' that," said Hale, his head turning a little on his arms, "is that! So can it, Israel! 'F yer *must* spout, do it in yer tit-fer… Wot abaht a bit o' moosic, Sawgint? … We're all layin' rahnd like a lot o' lumps o' Gawd-'elp-us tied up ugly… We *do* look 'appy! … 'appy as four old tarts at a meetin' o' virgins." He began to croon softly:

> "I wanter go 'ome,
>   Right er-way *h*over ther sea.
> I don' wanter go up ther line no more,
>   W'ere wizz-bangs an' sumpers arahnd me do roar.
> I wanter go 'ome

W'ere Johnny Turk can't get at me
Oh my! I don' wanter die-ee—
I-I-I wanter go 'o-ome…

Come on, you sons o' lidy dawgs! Chorust, please! All tergevver now…"

For the first lines only the Sergeant joined his voice to the nasal twang of the Cockney; then, on "whizz-bangs" Morelli came in. For the final mournful couplet with its wailing cadence, Abelson surprisingly lifted his voice.

The lingering "h-o-o-me" had barely died away before the Sergeant, his pleasant, deep baritone seeming a mere whisper which was yet musical and plain to hear, began to sing:—

"Some kiss, some bliss!
Some beauti-ful girl!
It was a dream of de-light…"

They joined him at once. The stickily yearning notes of that sticky waltz went lilting through the trees and died away with faint, faint echoes.

There is no sentimentalist to equal in saccharinity the fighting Jew. Abelson scrambled to his feet. His hoarse, harsh voice broke into "Annie Laurie." He stood in the moonlight and threw back his black, cropped head and the soft light played tricks with his fierce, sensual, heavy-jowled face with its leering mouth and satyr's nose.

The song was sung with all its stanzas; from the braes of Maxwelltoun to "for the sake o' Annie Laurie, I would lay me doon an' dee."

There was silence after that. But not for long. Abelson sat, but Hale stood. He said: "Very nicet. Ve-ry nicet! Hi will now give seelections from my reepertoyer:

> "'Old yer rah, 'old yer rah! …
> You ain't 'eard a word abaht 'arf wot's occurred…
> 'Old yer rah… wot d'yer sye?
> We're all clergyman's daughters wot lives dahn our wye."

They joined with him in the twenty odd stanzas, to which this was the chorus, going faithfully through the whole ironic melodrama. They came to an end of it and sat smiling.

Morelli, with a sudden bounce, got to his feet. There was still the shadow of his Jonahdom upon his broad, snub-nosed face, but behind and over it was now growing a smile. He tripped the Cockney neatly and rolled him upon his back. "Make way f'r your betters, London," he said. "Now, take the songs, *and* the time, from y'r uncle. And sit well back."

He began: "She was Poor but She was Honest, Victim of a Rich Man's Whim…" And as he sang he danced. They took his time. They sang with him, they marked that time with soft clappings. They saw a Morelli they had not known: they watched Morel, of Morel and Moree, Specialty Dancers.

He danced that song. He was the Poor and Honest Lady in all her phases, through all her scandalous adventures. He was the Rich Man; the Army Capting; Her Aged Parients. All the time he danced; his acting was in his feet, his little, square chunk of a body, which seemed now writhingly feminine, now bloatedly masculine, now mincing, now haughty... and all, every gesture, every movement, every step, pregnant with the subtle genius of the caricaturist.

He danced; they sang for him, laughter at times blurring words and tune. His interpretation of that verse which runs:

> "See 'im in the 'ouse o' Commons
>   Making laws to put down Crime...
> While the Victim of his Parshun
>   Walks home thru' the Mud and Slime..."

so worked upon Hale that he ceased to be part of the orchestra and lay upon his back and clucked.

The Sergeant, singing, and clapping at the beats, smiled round upon them. He sang:

> "In a Cottage in the Country
>   Where her Aged Parents live,
> They drink the Champagne what she sends 'em
>   *But* they never can Forgive."

Morelli came abruptly to a halt. This was the end of the song. He sat down.

They clapped, they begged for more. "Go on, Morry!" Abelson cried, beaming. "Caw! Caw!" said Hale. "Caw! Caw!"

The Sergeant felt something tugging at his sleeve. A low, shaking, urgent voice whispered in his ear. "Sergeant! Sergeant!" He jumped to his feet and saw in the deep shadow behind the trunk against which he had been leaning the dim figure of Sanders.

"What's up?" His tone was sharp, his voice low. Hale and Abelson and Morelli scrambled up and went to the tree against which leaned their rifles. They moved with the jerky swiftness of men whose nerves are on edge.

"Come on, man!" The Sergeant put a hand on the shadow's thin arm and shook it. Sanders came into the light of the clearing. "Come on, man!" said the Sergeant again.

"The… that singing…" The man's voice was so low that the words barely carried.

'What is it? Bell?" The Sergeant had dropped his curtness: his tone, now, was casual. Abelson drew near, after him Hale and Morelli. All fingered their rifles. Their smiles had gone. Back in their faces were the lines of strain and anger and bewilderment.

Sanders shook his head. "No, Sergeant," he said. "He is sleeping. Peacefully… but… but I heard the singing… and I came out… and I heard… the songs themselves." His voice was rising; rising with every word. Even the soft silver light did not quench the flaming of his pale eyes. His shoulders lost, suddenly, their droop and were held square and high. His voice mounted. He cried:

"Vile dancing! bawdy songs! A man dying *there*: two others dead, *there*! All of us near to death. Lechers... all of you! ... But it is not too late... I say, with all the passion of belief..." His voice shook and giant beads of sweat stood upon his face. "I say that it is not too late... God has mercy... God *is* mercy infinite... Pray! Pray for the souls of these two men who died in their vileness... Pray..."

The Sergeant's voice cut across the impassioned cry. "Sanders!" It had in it the rasping ring of the parade ground.

The man shivered, as one would shiver who was waked from sleep by a plunge into ice-cold water. The fire died out of the eyes, the rigidity from his body. He put a hand to his head as if in bewilderment. He took that hand down to look, amazed, at the glistening sweat upon its palm.

The Sergeant touched him on the shoulder. He said: "Get back to the hut. At once. Your post is with Corporal Bell. You should never have left it. Go back."

The man turned, slowly, like a sleep-walker... Abelson jumped forward. His dark face was twisted with darker rage. "You sod!" he said. "You bloody — —! You half-baked Saviour! God — me, but I'd like to crucify *you*, you —! Upside bloody down..." His voice was choked and thick, the hands which held the rifle shook so that the magazine rattled with a tinny sound.

The Sergeant caught him by the shoulder and pulled him round. "Be *quiet*!" he said. He pushed him away, "Another word from you..."

They watched while Sanders, like a man in liquor, shambled away and was lost in the shadow.

"Well!" came Hale's voice. "Strike me a flarin' ruby! … 'E's bugs… abserlootely moost!"

Abelson, the rage still black in his face, turned away and walked to the far side of the clearing, to where his folded blankets lay. They saw him spread them and lie, his head buried in his arms.

The Sergeant said: "He's right. Kip's the order."

"Nice endin' to our swarry," said Hale.

Morelli looked down, with twisted mouth, at the rifle in his hands. "Put the gust up *me*," he said. "Sod 'im! Thought something'd *happened*!" He walked off in search of his blankets. His head hung. His Jonahdom was with him again.

Hale watched him ruefully. He yawned and hitched his rifle to his shoulder by its sling. "'Night, Sergeant," he said…

The garrison slept.

X

THE Sergeant stood once more upon the end of the hut's roof. He held to his eyes the field-glasses taken from the dead subaltern, and with them, his view temporarily obstructed every here and there by palm trunks, swept the desert to the westward of the oasis.

It was half an hour past five, and the sun, on its upward course, was now darting diagonal stabs of fire over the palms behind him: he could feel the hot rays... hot and promising a heat to which this was nothing... striking his back even through the thick felt of the spine pad which began at his neck, buttoned to his shirt under the flap of the linen shade pendant from his helmet, and at its other end was looped to his belt.

The glasses had a crack across each of the lower lenses. He found it difficult to decide whether they were better than the naked eye. With neither glass nor eye, however, could he see aught but sand and sand and yet more sand. He sought vainly for some sign which should tell of a nullah, but found none...

Round the spring were the men, all save the sick Corporal who now, as for the last six hours, slept peacefully, not waking even when they had re-dressed his wound. There was no guard, the Sergeant having waived its necessity while he should remain on high; the Corporal, too, had been left while Sanders should bathe himself and eat.

The rank and file were thus together in one place for the first time since they had reached this doubtful haven. MacKay, seated, was carrying out the Sergeant's orders concerning food, cutting up into equal portions one tin of beef, taken from the pack-saddle in the hut. On an empty haversack beside him were piled seven of the large, hard biscuits which go, with bully beef, to make an iron ration. To his right, in a group, were Abelson and Hale and Sanders, who, bent over canvas water buckets, were washing themselves. The Cockney and the Jew were stripped to the waist; they used a new cake of yellow soap found in the haversack of the dead Pearson. Sanders washed in his shirt: he had no soap, but laboured with hands and water. Apart from this group and facing MacKay, were Cook and Morelli, shaving; Cook with grunts as the blunt "issue" razor ploughed through the stiff bristles which sprouted from his cheeks and massive chin; Morelli with many oaths as the wafer edge of his worn "safety" scraped from his face a mixture of hair and skin. Between them, on an inverted mess-tin, lay a very small piece of pink soap and a small and battered shaving brush.

A peaceful scene, idyllic almost. The troops at ease. *Some of the boys of the Gallant —th Behind the Lines.* The sun, though mounting, was not yet beating down into the clearing; there was, almost, a feeling of freshness in the air. MacKay, scrupulous over his division, whistled mournfully down at the beef. Hale, between splutters, hummed snatches of the songs they had been singing the night before. He began the dirge-like tune of the Poor but Honest Lady, and laughed his shrill cackle at the memory of Morelli's dancing. Morelli, the anguish of shaving past, wiped the soap from his face and gave advice to Cook.

"Don't go so bald-headed at it, you sailor! Dror and dror and dror: that's the answer."

"Ar!" said Cook, painfully scraping…

Only Abelson and Sanders were quiet; the one with sullen anger still in his dark face; the other with that habitual closelipped silence which seemed louder than speech.

The Sergeant, turning his eyes a moment from the desert, looked down and across at the clearing. He saw the group strangely foreshortened: they reminded him, so that he smiled, of a troupe of marionettes he once had seen; they had, watched at this angle and in the startlingly clear and brilliant light, those same hard, uncouth outlines; that slight disproportion which makes so charmingly for the grotesque.

He stayed a moment, watching. Then, as he was about to turn his eyes again to that waste of sand, there came a sudden and violent disturbance of that wooden, delightfully unnatural grouping.

The Sergeant bit his lip and cursed beneath his breath… He had seen Sanders, his bathing over, jerk himself rigidly upright, slip, stagger a second, and kick over the bucket in which he had been washing. A jet of water flew high, to soak the right leg of Abelson's drill breeches. The main body of water sped along the ground… to the Sergeant it had looked like a dark broad gigantic insect… It drenched the boot upon Abelson's right foot.

The Jew had straightened with a feline quickness, the lithe, deep muscles upon his white back flowing in now deepening, now disappearing ripples. He had looked down at his leg and then up at Sanders in one darting glance... He had taken a pace forward... His right arm had flashed...

Now Sanders lay in the water his own bucket had held. He lay limp and huddled. Over him stood Abelson, his forearms, first at the end of each, moving slightly, tentatively, delicately; like graceful, well-oiled pistons... The other men had stiffened as they stood or sat. Grotesquely, rather; still keeping in the Sergeant's eyes their marionetishness. Their heads had all turned at the dull yet crisp "flock" of the fist meeting the jaw. Their movements were arrested and held in that moment and so for yet other moments, so that it seemed as if they were pictures in a cinematograph film which has been suddenly stopped and has thus become a mere magic lantern show...

The Sergeant slipped the glasses into the left hip-pocket of his breeches. He cupped his hands about his mouth and sent out a roar. "MacKay!"

The group lost their woodenness. MacKay jumped to his feet and turned, looking upward across the clearing to the hut. The Sergeant waved an arm. "Here!" he called. He sat delicately, and delicately slid from the roof and dropped to the ground. MacKay arrived in haste.

"Up there!" said the Sergeant. "Keep a look-out. Yell if you see anything." He thrust the glasses into the man's hand and bent. "Up!" he said. "Right away." MacKay scrambled up on to his shoulders and thence to the roof.

The Sergeant ran through the trees toward the edge of the clearing, where now the men had closed in until they made a solid block, giving, in that place, the strange impression of a crowd. Abelson, his rage fanned by that sudden loosening of control, stooped suddenly and wound the fingers of his left hand in the shirt breast of the limp, lying figure. He pulled, and with the pull the upper half of Sanders body rose. But the man was still unconscious; his head lolled, the eyes closed, the left side of the jaw showing already the beginnings of puffiness and the dark, angry flush of congested blood.

"Yeh —!" said Abelson between his teeth. He went on pulling. "Yeh faking —!" He bent to meet the rising body, and his right arm drew back. "Get up, yeh —!" he said. "Get up an" fight! Or I'll…"

From behind the heavy hand of Cook fell upon his naked shoulder; a hard, square, blunt-fingered hand whose palm callouses rasped against the shoulder's soft flesh; a hand with red hair on its back like a paw. It wrenched him round, this hand, to face its owner. With a choking snarl he let Sanders fall and sprang back a foot, then forward. His left fist drove towards Cook's stomach… the red paws and great mahogany forearms dropped to guard… the Jew's right came home against the square chin of that square face with a sound deeper, louder, than it had against the jaw of Sanders.

The watchers drew in their breath. Cook did not move. He shook his head a moment, turned away, and began to pull at his shirt, bending a little to get it over his shoulders.

The Sergeant was upon them. He looked at them a moment without speaking, his eyes going swiftly from face to face. He nodded towards Sanders on the ground. "He all right?" he said.

Morelli knelt beside the huddled body. As he peered into the face, greyly pale beneath its tan save for the jaw's livid patch, the eyelids flickered.

"O.K.," he said.

"Put him in the shade. Over there." The Sergeant pointed. "Chuck some water on his head."

Morelli dragged the limpness away, its boots trailing and raising little spurts of dust.

The Sergeant looked at Abelson. The smouldering eyes, now with little red flicks in their darkness, met his defiantly.

"You," asked the Sergeant, "and Cook?" He turned. "Cook!" he called.

Cook put the last neat fold to his khaki shirt, which he now set down upon the top of his helmet, lying by MacKay's biscuitladen haversack. He came heavily forward, tightening his belt.

"Ar?" he said.

The Sergeant sent his eyes from one to the other of the two: Abelson, slightly over middle height, with a body whose poise and grace and contours were delight to the eyes and whose skin, against the deep red-brown of neck and forearms, black-brown of the face and the blue-black of the brows and bullet-head, shone startlingly white; Cook, an inch the lower, square, solid, unbeautiful, with great muscles in gnarled and awkward-seeming lumps, with a thatch of reddish hair coating chest and breasts and half the stomach, with tattooings in crude but faded colours all about his arms and neck and beneath the red-brown thatch.

The Sergeant spoke. "Weight?" he said.

"Eleven-two!" growled Abelson.

Cook scratched his head.

"Twelve or thereabouts?" said the Sergeant. "Little more, p'r'aps."

"Ar," Cook nodded.

The Sergeant thrust his hands deep into his breeches pockets. He stood between them, swaying gently back and forth, heel and toe. He said:

"Now listen. Abelson, you've no business to go cuttin' loose. 'F it happens again, I'll put you under close arrest. Get me? I mean that; whatever our position is. Now, you two want to fight. You can, this time. It'll clear the air. But you're either going to fight as I say, or not at all. Get that? … Right… This do's goin' to be under Queensberry rules… Know 'em, Abelson?"

The Jew shook his head savagely.

"They're the rules," the Sergeant said, "that the Marquess of Queensberry made for the old pugs. Listen! … There 're rounds; but not by time. Wrestlin' throws are allowed. Rounds end when one of the men's down. One minute intervals… You can have ten of those." He glanced up at the sky. "Sun's not near high yet. 'F you start now you won't get the tap by bein' in the buff… Ten rounds, see? Or a K.O… Under these rules you're out if you can't come up, after your going down's made the end of the round, at the end of the minute's rest… One knee, or more of you, on the ground is down and therefore the end of a round ... Got that, both of you?"

"Ar," said Cook.

The Jew began to speak angrily. "What the hell..." he began.

The Sergeant cut him short. "Quiet! As I say, or not at all. 'Member that... What d'you think I am, Abelson? ... I know you... one of the best of the young middles... I'm having Queensberry's to make it a scrap an' not a procession... Your ancestors didn't mind 'em... What about Mendoza? He was half your size and a lunger... He fought this way... *and* worse... with men twice the size of Cook..."

"All *right*!" Abelson grumbled. "On'y let's cut this out and get busy..."

The Sergeant took his hands from his pockets. He stepped back. "Right," he said. "There's no ring for you. And not enough of us to make one. Keep in the middle here 's much 's you can. Hale, you look after Abelson. Morelli, you after Cook. I'm timekeeper... for the intervals... and ref. Stand back, Hale and Morelli..." They stood back, eagerly. "You two get away from each other...

"Right? ... Get to it..." He jumped back a pace...

Under the tree to which Morelli had dragged him, Sanders slowly struggled up until he sat. His eyes were fogged; they gazed mistily about him. He was shaken with a fit of vomiting.

XI

THE two stood facing each other, perhaps ten feet apart. The clearing was flooded with the light of the newly-risen sun, which pierced now horizontally through the fringing trees. In this pure blaze, so different from the blinding glare to come, their bodies, stripped to the waist, shone and glistened, with the sweat which broke out upon a man with every movement even at this the day's coolest hour, like the sleek and shining fur of two white seals.

Cook was square and upright, his right foot a little advanced, his fists together, the forearms at right angles with the biceps and parallel to the ground; he looked immensely thick and solid and permanent… entirely without fear or excitement.

Abelson by contrast was a nobleman's sword faced with the bludgeon of a giant sans-culotte… He stood upon the balls of his feet, erect and edgeways, his legs well apart. He presented to his enemy the very least possible target. His left arm slid in and out, slightly, with a lithe, sure flicker; his right was still, slanting down, from fist to elbow, across his body. His face was tucked down behind that white left shoulder, so that only his eyes showed above it, dark and malignant and watchful. His stance was, in essence, that of the old-time stylists; but with the great difference that it was not taut and rigid. His every movement was flowing and effortless and swift as a cat; he could… would, probably… change this style for another so often and so quickly as suited his purpose.

He drew closer, imperceptibly, breaking this way and that with light, dancing, economical steps seemingly unhindered by the heavy service boots upon his feet. Cook was motionless... only his blue eyes, bright under the shaggy, down-drawn red brows, shifted their gaze to follow the dark ones peering over that protecting shoulder...

Abelson feinted with his body to the right; then as suddenly to the left... Cook's double guard shifted sympathetically... There was a sudden flurry of movement and the sound of two blows, so close together as to be almost one sound... Cook shook his massive head and snorted twice: Abelson danced back out of reach, his full red lips twisted into a sneering smile. Beneath Cook's left eye a slow trickle of blood started; a dull dark flush spread itself over his right ear.

The Jew was away for only the barest second. In he came again. Cook let fly a right... a surprisingly swift blow for so seemingly slow a man. Abelson did not check his advance; his knees bent, very slightly, and the great fist brushed light over his hair... Then he was in; his fists beat a tattoo upon the ribs and stomach... He danced out again...

Hale, standing with Morelli, pursed his lips in a soundless whistle. "'E may be a bleedin' Buckle, but 'e *can* scrap! Eh, Morey? Pore ole Matlow!"

Morelli shrugged. "Maybe. Wish Cookie would hit 'im, just once!"

The twisted, sneering smile was wide upon the Jew's face. He came close, not dancing now, and stood. He had, apparently, no guard. Cook struck, with left and right. Again the blows were surprisingly quick... But not quick enough. Abelson ducked the first, with a graceful, inward-sliding movement of the upper part of his body. He deflected the second with a gliding push of his left arm... He was close in now... He drove in four incredibly rapid, shattering six-inch punches, all just over the heart... He ducked out again, snapped erect and got home, one immediately following the other, a right cross, over Cook's shoulder, to the jaw, and, as this punch swung its target round, a flashing left upper-cut which brought quick blood from Cook's lower lip.

"Oh — it!" whispered Hale. "'Taint a scrap at all... A bleedin' slaugher-'ouse do!"

Morelli dismally nodded.

The fight went on... always Abelson attacked, never in the same way but ever achieving the same result. Cook, despite the bruise beneath his left eye, the swollen ear, the cut lip, seemed untroubled. His position was unchanged, his breathing unhurried, his eyes serenely watchful.

"But 'e *must* feel *them*," Hale said beneath his breath. "'Emust! They ain't no slap-an'-tickles, believe me!"

Then, in a flash the unexpected... Abelson darted in on another of his raids... Cook, instead of standing his ground dropped his head and his hands, and rushed forward to meet the attack. A hard left, meant for his face, cracked harmless on his poll… and then his great, knotted arms were round the Jew, about his arms and body…

"Whee!" said Morelli. "*That's* the stuff, Cookie! Good old Queensberry!"

"*Blime!*" breathed Hale. "Looka there!"

The great arms were squeezing, squeezing… The Jew's dark face had lost its smile; it wore now a startled look… the look of a man who has put his foot upon a non-existent step. His mouth was a round O, his eyes two more… The grip inexorably tightened, and he grunted with the pain of the constriction…

"Looka there, I tell yer!" Hale danced on one foot in his excitement.

For Cook was straightening his crouching body… The Jew's feet were off the ground… an inch… two inches… a clear half foot. Cook was now nearly erect … He suddenly stiffened, twisted, thrust a column of a leg forward and outward… Abelson, helpless, was caught in the small of his back by the top of that thigh and fell, sprawling heavily.

He lay a moment, the breath beaten out of him, his head and body shaken by the force of his fall. Cook turned and walked away: Morelli, hastening to meet him, set down the half-full canvas bucket which he carried and dropped upon one knee; on the other Cook sat, placid and bulky.

Abelson, the surprise in his face giving way before rage, scrambled to his feet. He seemed about to hurl himself across the intervening yards at the seated Cook, now splashing water over his head and face.

"End o' the round!" The Sergeant stepped forward. "Three-quarters of a minute left, Abelson. Better rest... Hale 'll look after you." He kept his eyes upon the second hand of his watch.

Hale came, bucket in hand, his face empty of expression. Abelson waved him away. He would not rest: he would have no ministration. The dull red flecks had returned to the dark eyes. He paced, impatient, up and down, muttering beneath his breath. The white, gleaming skin of his body was white and gleaming no longer; grey, thick dust befouled it. His breathing came deep and hard and loud... The sweat ran down his breasts and down his back, carving channels of white through the clinging thick filth.

"Time!" called the Sergeant.

With a spring more feline yet than any of his always feline movements, Abelson leapt. Cook was barely on his feet in time to meet the onslaught... He steadied himself and crouched and wrapped his arms about his head, bending to meet the storm.

The Jew, though rage held him, was yet too excellent a boxer to lose altogether his judgment. He did not rain blows, after his first leads, on that bent head and guarding arms. He stepped back; he crouched himself, so low that it almost seemed as if his knees must scrape the ground. He waited...

Cook, peering through these crossed arms, began to straighten himself... Abelson, still crouching, came on like a whirlwind... He drove blows at the body, short, twisting, driving punches... He was close... he stayed close, while he hammered... Cook, grunting under this rain, straightened fully. He flung out his arms, hands open, clutching... The Jew slid from under them as water through the tines of a fork... Cook pursued... He swung a right, a blow which then, had it landed, would have ended this fight.

But it did not land. Swiftly, neatly, with an insolent ease, the Jew side-stepped. Cook blundered past him, carried on by the force of his own punch. He got, as he shot past, almost falling, a smashing downward left, which landed behind his right ear... He fell, heavily, forward on to his face... Abelson stood over him, his right arm drawn back, his left flickering in and out, in and out, tentative, feeling ... Cook stirred... He began to raise himself, slowly, upon his arms. The Jew's right arm drew farther back...

The Sergeant jumped forward. He put a heavy hand upon Abelson's shoulder and pulled him back. He said:

"End o' the round... Remember what I told you... Stand right back... Right away from him... There's a minute now!"

Sullenly the Jew dropped his hands and turned slowly away. Hale came to him. "Water?" he said. "Wanter knee?"

"—yer knee!" Abelson snatched at the bucket, set it down and scooped water from it with his hands. He bathed his face and neck. "What sort o' scrap's this?" he said. "Fancy — rules! 'Tain't fightin' at all..."

Hale was silent. From the corner of his eye he watched Cook, helped by Morelli, get stiffly to his feet, his face covered with dust which now had caked black upon blood and sweat. He sat heavy on Morelli's knee and rubbed and dabbed at this filth with the handkerchief Morelli had soaked in the bucket. His movements were slow and listless. His eyes bent themselves blankly on the ground.

Abelson paced feverishly about. His lips moved unceasingly in thick and silent cursing. The dust of his fall still clung to his back and powdered gray the cropped black of his hair...

"Time!" called the Sergeant.

Again Abelson leapt. But this time he had not so far to go. Incredibly, Cook, too, at that call of the Sergeant's, had waked to sudden furious life. His head down, bull-like, he rushed. And, bull-like, his speed was unexpected and astonishing.

They met with a thud. Abelson, for once thrown off his guard by sheer surprise, met this unexpectedness with a light left lead. Cook, snorting, took the blow in his stride ... Once more the great arms clamped themselves round the arms and trunk of his opponent.

"That's the stuff!" Morelli shouted. "Atta Matlow!"

"Quiet!" said the Sergeant.

It seemed, at first, that there was to be a repetition of that throw which had brought an end to the first round ... It was clear that Abelson thought this. He strained, contorting his face with the effort, to keep his feet upon the ground... Suddenly he was released... He stood alone...

For one fatal second, this miracle filled him with amazement… He stood, arms hanging at his sides, eyes staring incredulous…

Cook had stepped back half a pace… His right fist, the punch travelling upward from his hip, took the Jew just beneath the curving juncture of the breast-bone… The blow resounded. It was a ringing, hollow report, that clapped on the watchers' ears… Instinctively they drew in their breath with little hisses…

At that terrific blow, paralyzing the nerve-centre called the solar-plexus, the Jew crumpled. All the blood left his face, which shone suddenly ash-grey. His mouth fell open, the lower jaw sagging grotesquely. His knees, slowly, gave beneath him. He began to topple forward, crumpling as he fell…

Cook shifted his stance a little… He measured his distance with a careful eye… As the Jew was falling, he hit him again… His left fist landed, with another ringing, heavy report, just below the right ear, over the carotid…

The direction of Abelson's falling changed. Instead of crumling forwards, he was straightened again… as if a spring within him had been released… and fell, still straight, crashing heavily upon his left shoulder… He rolled over and lay still as the sand itself, face downwards. A small dust cloud raised itself above him.

The Sergeant flicked open his watch. He called: "Hale! Try an' bring him round! Do y'r damndest… He's got a minute…"

Hale flung himself forward. He sat and took the Jew's head on his knee. He poured water on the grey face, with its closed eyes. He flicked at the now flaccid cheeks… He worked hard and well. He had seconded men before this.

His efforts were unrewarded by even so much as a flicker of the closed eyelids. He massaged the muscles of the stomach and succeeded in making the breathing more regular. But it remained stertorous. The Sergeant had his eyes fixed on his watch. Over half of the minute now had passed. Hale tried his last card: he jerked more water over the unheeding head, then lifted it and bent his own to meet it.

He took the lobe of Abelson's right ear between his teeth and bit hard… an old trick of the good second… but the pain passed Abelson by… His body still was utterly limp… in it there was no movement nor shadow of movement.

"Time!" The Sergeant closed his watch with a snap. He walked across and stood by Hale, looking down at the Jew. "He *is* out!" he said. Hale nodded… Together they carried the limp body back and into the shade of the trees. "Good job it's over," said the Sergeant. "Another five minutes and I'd 've had to stop it… The sun 'd've been right up and coming slick down on 'em."

In the clearing, Cook, a full bucket at his feet, was bathing the sweat from his body and the blood and dust from his face. Morelli, ecstatic, hovered round him, glancing up every now and then at the sun, just appearing over the top of the fringe of palms. He said anxiously:

"Come *on*, Cookie. You'll get a Doolally in a minute. Put y'r shirt an' spine-pad an' cadie on, f'r Chrisake! Or come in the shade… Feelin' O.K.?"

Cook brushed the water with both hands from his hair. "Ar!" he said.

XII

THE Sergeant walked among the palms. "Sanders!" he called; and again: "Sanders!" He walked on, more quickly now. His eyes roved from side to side.

He came to a sudden halt. He peered, blinked, and looked again. Relief smoothed the sharper lines momentarily from his face. There was Sanders; he knelt beside the trunk of a palm. A low gabble came to the Sergeant's ears. Closer, he could hear the words, spoken in a voice low and controlled, but yet strangely giving the impression of a shout. He halted, walked on, halted again... He was so close now that another step would have taken him on top of the praying man. The sharp lines came back into his face. He tilted his topee forward over his eyes and rubbed meditatively at the back of his head.

"... O Lord of Mercy!" said the voice of Sanders. "Hear this thy abased and humble Servant! ... I supplicate Thee, O Lord! Grant that a single gem from the Crown of Thy Grace may fall upon this spot and cast its Light into the Souls of these Men gathered here upon it... may soften and cleanse and beautify Them... may plant in Their Evil hearts the Seed of that Divine plant which shall lead them to Thee, even in this hour when Death is hard upon Them..."

The Sergeant turned. He walked slowly away, still rubbing, meditative, with his palm at the back of his head. The voice grew faint in his ears... fainter... died away.

He came out into the clearing. In the shade beyond its farther edge sat Cook and Morelli and Hale. Ten yards to their right, alone, sat Abelson. He had been recovered now, after that ten minutes of unconsciousness, for half an hour. He sat huddled, his knees drawn up and round them his arms. He gazed with blank dark eyes from a face of misery.

The Sergeant walked across the clearing and past him and on to where sat the three. He said:

"Morelli, there's no one with Corporal Bell. I've just left him. Cut along and into the hut for a bit. You all right, Cook?"

"Ar," said Cook, and nodded.

"Hale," said the Sergeant, "rummage up a bit of paper. Cut it into six strips, five short, one long."

Hale got to his feet. "This the dror?" he asked. "Wot O!" He walked off across the clearing and bent over the haversack of the dead Pearson.

The Sergeant went to Abelson and stood looking down at him. "You all right?" he said.

The Jew growled something in his throat. He looked down, so that the brim of his topee hid his face.

"Sure?" asked the Sergeant.

Abelson's helmet still hid the face beneath it. "'Course I'm all right!" he said. His voice was an octave higher than its usual pitch: it trembled and was choked like that of a child trying under stress to be grown-up.

"Think I've never been hit before?" he said. "Goddlemighty! that's my job... that an' hittin' the other feller. Take a sight more than two raps from *that* slab-sided — to reely hurt *me*..." He jerked his head in Cook's direction.

"— him!" he said, and choked. "— his bloody soul, the Gentile's bahstud!"... He abandoned pretence and openly laid his head upon the arms that now he had crossed upon his drawn-up knees.

The Sergeant looked down at him. He said, after a pause:

"Pull yourself together, Abelson. This won't do! Forget it!"

"Forget it!" The Jew's voice cracked on its high note. "*Forget it!*" He raised his head, tilting it to look up into the Sergeant's face. His eyes, wide and dark, glittered bright with unshed tears. "I'll never fight again!" he said. "'F I get back, I'll be a... a waiter or a fishmonger's office boy... or a pimp... Thassall I'm fit for... Getting put out by a soor's choot that never did anythin' 'cept rough-house cabin-boys..."

"Should've thought," said the Sergeant, "you'd take a hiding better than this. What about the time Kid Walker put you out at Premierland? Seventh round."

"Well, what about it?" Abelson's tone was fierce, the voice lower now but throaty as he swallowed at that lump which seemed to choke him. "Did I mind *that*? Did I *Hell*! That was a *scrap*... An' Hookey Walker's the best ever ... or was then; he wasn't boozing in them days... Honour to be put out by Hookey... An' you gotter remember he was twenty-five then an' *I* was sixteen... Yessir, s-i-x-teen, that was me... But, anyway, *that* was a scrap, an' I was beat 'cos he was better'n me... See? ... It was a *fight*; not a bleedin' ketch-as-ketch-can huggin'-party with a lot o' all-me-eye rules made up on the spot... Get me? ...

Oh, *I* know... Yeh says yeh wanted to make it *fair!*"
... He scrambled suddenly to his feet and stood facing the
Sergeant. The dark eyes blazed brighter, the face was distorted, the lips drawn back rigid from the white teeth in an
effort to keep them from trembling.

"*Fair!*" he said. "An' I got beat by a bloody great oaf like
that! ... I'll never fight again... It's not... it's not..." He
turned sharply on his heel and walked away.

"Abelson!" called the Sergeant. "Over to the hut, right
away." His voice was now the impersonal trumpet of
authority.

"Cook!" he called. "Hale! Over to the hut." He turned
and led the way. They struggled after him, rifles in the
crooks of their arms.

The sun now bore down full into the clearing. Its heat
smote them like a physical blow. Hale gasped a little. "Like
bein' a sossidge in 'ell!" he said. "On'y wants a fork through
y'r guts an' there y'are!"

"Ar!" said Cook. He puffed out his lips and worked his
face in strange grimaces. The salt sweat which broke out
on a man's every movement was stinging the cuts and
bruises left by the fists of Abelson.

They came to the trees again and the sun did not strike
them unprotected. Hale dug his elbow into the ribs of
Cook beside him.

"Dekko!" He pointed ahead to where Abelson, alone,
was nearing the hut. He walked strangely, with a curiously
stiff back and rigid inclination of the head. Hale gave his
cackle. "Neck's like a poker! 'Twasn't arf a snorter you

give 'im, Matlow." He laughed again. "Pore old Isaacstein: walkin' like a ruddy nymp' wiv 'Ousemaid's Shoulder."

They came to the hut and stood about its doorway, leaning on their rifles. Above them, on the roof, stood MacKay.

"Matlow," he said, "yon waur a rare wallopin' ye gied the Levite. Ah couldna *keep* lookin', y'understan', but Ah neglekit ma duty every ither once an' a while… Ah seen those bonny, bonny slaps…"

The Sergeant came out of the hut's dark mouth. "That'll do, MacKay!" he said. "Hale, got those slips?"

The Cockney put his hand to his breeches pocket and brought forth six neatly-torn pieces of pink notepaper. "Pearson's," he explained. "'E 'ad a ruddy stationer's stock o' coggage in 'is 'aversack… Always writin' to 'is Mar, 'e was, pore little squit…"

The Sergeant took the paper. "Get round," he said. "Come on, Abelson… Now: you can all see these? … I'm goin' to fold 'em, so!" He doubled up each strip into a compact little wad, differing not at all from its fellows. He dropped them one by one into Bell's green-lined topee, which hung by its chin-strap over his arm. "We'll draw now… You know what it's for… The man that gets the long strip chooses his own half-section… I'll shake 'em up, so… Anyone any objections 'bout the way this is being done? … No… Right. Hale, you hold the topee … We'll draw alphabetically, me last…" He lifted his voice: "MacKay, let Cook draw for you, in your turn?"

"Ay!" came down from the roof.

"Right." He turned his head, to see Morelli emerging from the door behind him. "There you are... Hear that? Agree?"

Morelli nodded. Hale took the helmet between his hands; cautiously, as a man might hold a bowl of treasured glass. They looked, all of them, at this helmet. There was an utter silence...

"Abelson!" The Sergeant's voice cut into the stillness.

The Jew came forward. He walked slowly, his head held still at that stiff and awkward angle. He stood a moment, looking up from the ground on which his eyes had been fixed. He seemed about to speak; but did not. He put his hand down into that helmet and brought from it one of the little pink wads.

"Keep it like that," said the Sergeant. "Cook!" Cook dipped. "Now yourself, Hale. That's right... Now Cook for MacKay's, and keep those two distinct... Morelli ..." He came close himself now and took between his fingers the last little lump of paper. "Right away," he said. "Unroll 'em."

There was silence again, broken by a little, concerted rustling which rattled on their ears loud as machine-gun fire...

"Ar!" came the voice of Cook. He held up the long strip.

"Your own?" said the Sergeant.

Cook nodded solemnly.

"Up to you now, Cook." The Sergant came forward to face him. "Choose your sidekicker."

"Who wud it be but ma'sel'?" MacKay's voice came down, urgent, to their ears.

"Ar!" Cook look up, a great grin split suddenly his square, battered face; as suddenly went.

"Ah told ye!" came the voice from above them again. "Ah told ye, Sergeant. What use was there in yon pheenanderin'? Ah said Ah'd be goin', an' there ut is!"

The Sergeant looked up at him. "You'd better come down off your perch then." He turned to the men about him and stood a moment scanning their faces. They were blank, these faces. Unreadable. "Hale," he said.

"Sawgint?"

"Relieve MacKay. And keep those eyes of yours peeled… Yell if there's anything. Morelli'll take over in an hour. We'll have reliefs on this job… Through the day… Nights 'll be as before. Won't do to be up there at night: wouldn't see as much as on the level. Not with those shadows."

There was a scrambling rush, and MacKay stood with them, "Up wi' ye, London," he said, and made a back. Hale, like a thick, tall monkey, scrambled and clawed his way and presently stood upon the roof, glasses at his eyes.

"An' *now*," said MacKay, "you an' me, we'll be needin' to haver, Serrgeant." He smiled and was jigging on his feet. He pushed back his topee and wiped with a damp forearm at the sweat glistening upon his lined face and running down his forehead from the roots of the silver hair. "It's hotter'n Satan 'ud believe, up yon!" he said.

XIII

THE sun rose high, higher. It blazed down, its molten stream pouring vertically upon the desert and upon this island in the desert's barrenness... It waned, sliding slowly and cruelly down its slope, fighting every inch to retain its majesty... It dipped, blazed out awhile in strange and wild and poignant colours... It went.

The moon bathed the world, pouring a quiet and silver balm over the tortured surface of the waste, which now began to throw upward, as a fevered man will heave at his blankets, the heat which for those endless-seeming hours had been bearing down upon and into it.

The trees of the oasis again were black cardboard against a silver lime. The little spring, whose noise by day seemed strangely to be hushed, again made its plashing heard, sounding coolly in the ears of the men who stood about it.

They were five: the Sergeant, Cook, MacKay, Hale, and Morelli. Pacing a beat extending over the western side of the oasis was Abelson; he carried his rifle at the slope; his eyes searched, dark and restless, the gleaming sand upon which nothing moved for so far as the eye could reach. In the hut, where the heat of all the days seemed prisoned, Sanders sat by the side of the wounded Corporal.

There was a silence by the spring. The group stood, the men shifting uneasily upon their feet. The Sergeant fumbled at the watch upon his wrist. Cook, unmoved, settled more easily about him his strange equipment: a bandolier of ammunition, two low-hung and bulging haversacks, in them three days' supply of meat and biscuit; one of the water-sacks that had used to go upon the pack-horse strapped (infantry-packwise and about a third part full) across his back. MacKay, beside him, changed and re-changed the slack of the slings on the two rifles which he was to carry: over his left shoulder, in addition to his bandolier, was the band of a haver-sack which held a thick, pressed-together mass of dates plucked that afternoon; over his right the bands of two laden water-bottles. In his right hip-pocket was the map, neatly folded.

The silence continued. An uneasy, loud silence.

MacKay broke it. He gave a last decisive hitch at the rifle slings; looked down and about himself at his equipment; patted his left breeches-pocket to ensure that the compass was there. He turned to Cook behind him. "Are ye ready, Matlow?" he said. His words shattered the silence as if a voice were something new and strange and rather terrible.

"Ar!" said Cook.

MacKay said, half-interrogatively: "We'll be makin' a start then, Serrgeant."

"Er… right!" The Sergeant was still, but his voice was that of a man who suddenly has shaken his shoulders to ease them of a strain which he knows will not be eased. He stepped forward and held out his hand. He said:

"So long, Jock. Good luck."

The hands of the venturers were shaken by everyone. MacKay became voluble. He answered, with slow and rather heavy and very Scottish facetiousness the variations of the Sergeant's "So long: good luck" that were pressed upon him. Cook was silent, merely nodding his great head, with its bruised face, and smiling.

The Sergeant became again Authority. "Hale! Morelli! Join Abelson on the other side there. Tell him to stop patrollin'. Get right at the edge of the trees, the three of you; lie down 'bout ten yards apart, and *watch*. I'm stayin' this side for a bit. Jildi now!"

They went, trotting, their rifles horizontal in their right hands, their bandoliers swinging and jolting across their shoulders. They disappeared among the black-latticed shadows of the trees.

The Sergeant, between MacKay and Cook, walked through the trees upon the eastern side and so to the top of the slope leading down on that side to the sand of the desert. He said:

"Got everything? Map, compass, grub, ammunition, pawny? And that paper with the route we calculated?"

MacKay nodded. "Matlow!" he said, "here we go! Guid nicht to ye, Serrgeant. We'ull be sendin' along for ye shortly: four-five days. Maybe sinner."

The Sergeant smiled. He said; "We'll look out for you."

He stood, rifle in hand, watching the two as they scrambled down the shadowed slope and so on to the silver, black-blotched floor of the desert. They trudged stolidly on, their khaki helmets shining in the moonlight like pantomime armour. They had gone perhaps four hundred yards when the slighter figure, MacKay, turned in his walk and waved an arm. The Sergeant came down from out

MacKay turned in his walk and waved an arm.

the trees and waved response. The figure turned to tramp ahead by the side of its companion.

The Sergeant climbed the slope again and stood leaning against the trunk of the outermost palm. His eyes roved to this side and that, covering the great flat, infinite half-circle before him; coming back, every half-minute or so, to the two toiling figures.

They grew smaller, these figures. At first they remained sharp, clear-cut, black against the sheet of silver beneath their feet; merely, to the Sergeant's eye, growing shorter and shorter. Then, with a very gradual transition, the sharpness went; for a time the figures, now tiny, retained their size, while the clean-cut edges thickened and blurred and misted...

Then he could only see one speck... Right away, far in the distance, a black speck, occasionally seeming to split into two, which receded and receded.

Then he could see nothing... nothing but the gleaming sand, with every here and there those dark, leprous blotches of unreasonable shadow.

His eyes, weary of straining, began to play him false. A blurry mist came over them, and a film of fatigue. He rubbed at them; then turned away and walked back through the trees to the edge of the clearing. He cupped his hands about his mouth and called, on a low, deep note:

"Mor-elli!"

A low hail came back to his ears; and, after a moment, to his eyes Morelli's square, short figure which ran towards him.

The Sergeant held up a hand. "Asti, asti!" he said.

Morelli came up panting. "Yes, Sergeant?"

"Take it easy, man." The Sergeant smiled. "I want you this side; that's all. Nothing over there?"

Morelli pulled a wry mouth. "Fanny Adams! 'cept sand… Wish for Chrisake somep'n *would* bob up… Better 'n this wait, wait, *and* wait… Get's on a guy's nerves."

The Sergeant ignored this small outburst. "There's four of us now, leaving out Sanders, who seems to want to stay on the nurse's job. To-night we'll take two-hour reliefs of two, right through. One man this side, one the other. Patrol and meet at the north and south ends every now and then if you want to. Abelson'll stay on with you. Hale and I take over in two hours." He nodded and walked off across the clearing and gave again his directions.

Hale walked back at his side, towards the hut. He said, in a sudden little burst of words:

"Jock an' the Matlow's orf, then… wot jer reckon, Sarge? Think as 'ow they'll pull it off? Eh, Sarge? Think as they'll find the Brigyde… or some of our blokes? 'Ow far you say it was? Sixty-seventy mile? Kerist! Wot a toddle… But them's a coupla good 'uns… Looka, Sarge, you ever *see* such a coupla wallops 's Cookie slipped ole Circumcision… Phe-ew! … S'pose they does get froo, Sarge… oughta be back…"

The Sergeant cut deliberately across this spate of words. He said:

"Tell you what I think: they've got a good chance. Now chubbarow and help me build a fire. We've got to make more soup for Bell."

Hale, still talking, disappeared among the trees where the slight undergrowth was thickest. The Sergeant looked after him, a frown creasing his forehead. The man's voice had been high and jerky and excited; the blithe and sardonic and caustic humour had been absent; the legs had been... or was it a trick of his tired eyes? ... wavering ever so slightly; the stream of talk had been feverish and disconnected and quite unlike the...

"Nerves!" thought the Sergeant. "Or p'r'aps not. Possibly my own."

Hale came back with kindling of a sort and some larger pieces. He was quiet now, and slow and lethargic. They built a fire: its smoke rose straight in the leaden air. Hale crouched dejected beside it, feeding to it, every now and then, pieces of fuel. The Sergeant entered the hut.

A wave of air, hotter even than the oven breath without, hit him in the face like a heavy, soft blow. There were sounds, too, in the darkness. Bell twisted weakly, uneasy in his sleep, and mumbled and muttered words and fragments of words emerged once in a while startlingly, boldly clear from the soft and fevered incoherences surrounding them. By his blankets, a dim, squat shape in the darkness, crouched Sanders. He too was speaking; rapidly, softly.

The Sergeant stood a moment silent in the doorway.

"... the bitch..." came clear in the hoarse, creaking voice of the wounded man. Mumble... mumble... "God rot her eyes..." The mumble rose in volume; became a thick, dark stream of inarticulate vehemence. It died away quite suddenly.

Then the murmured words of Sanders: "… this troubled soul, O God! Grant that it may find solace in…"

The Sergeant went on and into the hut. "Sanders!" he said softly.

The shape rose to meet him. "Yes?" it whispered.

"Get outside," said the Sergeant. He went to the pack-saddle in the far corner and from it took a tin of beef, leaving only three. With the tin in his hand he groped his way to the door and went out again into the moonlight.

Beside the hut, over the now blazing little fire, Hale still crouched. At the other side stood Sanders. The Sergeant went to them. "Get that mess-tin, Sanders," he said.

The man held it out. "I imagined that you would want it. Is there anything else you wish. Or shall I go back… in there?" He motioned with his head towards the doorway behind him.

The Sergeant took the mess-tin and laid it upon the ground. He sat himself down beside it and took his jack-knife from his pocket. He began opening the tin of beef. He said:

"No. I want to speak to you. He's worse… isn't he?"

"He seems feverish. He has been… delirious," Sanders said slowly. A sudden spurt of flame from the little fire showed his face, bleak and thin and fanatic, to the Sergeant's upward-peering eyes.

"I heard him, Sanders… And you." The voice of Authority was cloaked in velvet, but not disguised. "I want to tell you… if you want to pray, do it quietly. Understand? Don't make any noise near that poor devil… Now you have an easy… You've had a bad day. I'll look after him for an hour or so, until I go on guard… How's your jaw? Hurt much?"

Sanders' body, thin and meagre and ill-befitting its militant clothes, drew sharply erect. His bare, narrow head was striped with silver bars and black from the palm-filtered moon; a red glow from the fire bathed his arms and torso. He said, in a voice tight and strained and so low that barely was it audible:

"I have no discomfort." But his hand crept up to his cheek, the fingers feeling tenderly at the side of the jaw between chin and ear.

The Sergeant became brusque. "Right," he said. "Now do what you like. Have an easy, man! Go and wash or sleep or smoke… Let yourself out a bit." He watched covertly while Sanders, stiffly erect, wheeled and marched off, with the uncouth gait of a raw recruit endeavouring vainly to emulate the seasoned soldier. He followed with his eyes until the awkward figure was lost in the shadows; then turned to the opening of the tin. He said:

"Feelin' O.K., Hale?"

"So-so." The Cockney's voice was flat and limp and dreary. "It's so *bleeding* 'ot… Wot I want's a woman! … A nicet little brown 'un, I'd like…"

The Sergeant smiled. "Supply and demand don't always work out. Demand like hell; but the supply of bibis wouldn't come off… not in this hole." He scooped out half of the limp mass of meat, pouring on to the ground the melted grease. He placed the meat in the mess-tin. "Get a drop o' water, will you?" he said. "Bottleful."

Hale got up stiffly to his feet. He stretched slowly, his hands pressed to the small of his back, which ached. He bent and rubbed at his thighs, for they ached too. He went off, heavily, in search of the spring and his water-bottle.

The Sergeant put down, carefully, the mess-tin. He got to his feet and tiptoed to the hut's doorway and listened. He heard the heavy, quick breathing of the sick man; then a mutter of thick sounds: then, quite clearly:

"… please… for God's sake…" The coherence went and there came again the wild, half-whispered, half-shouted babble. The Sergeant waited while his eyes might become accustomed to the darkness… He knelt at last beside the huddled figure on the blankets. He put a hand upon the sick man's forehead: the skin was parched and dry and burning. He groped and found a water-bottle, half full. He slipped his left arm under the man's neck and uncorked the bottle with his teeth.

"… you bleedin' sow! …" The words burst from the head upon his arm. "You whore… standin' there… Gimme that glass… jildi… It's not *you* I want…"

The Sergeant brought the neck of the bottle gently to the burning, babbling lips. Against his forearm the stiff hairs of the unshaven shin rasped and scratched…

By the spring Hale painfully stooped and trapped water in the narrow neck of his bottle. Three yards from him, unheeding, lay Sanders. He was prone, his head buried in his arms.

Hale straightened from his task with a groan. That ache in his back grew intense. He became aware that he was not sweating. He looked at Sanders, lying. "Oy!" he called, and again: "Oy!"

Sanders raised his head. He said wearily, "Yes? What is it?"

Hale went slowly across and stood looking down at him. "Wot's the *matter*?" he said. "Fer the love o' *Mike*, cheer up... Fice 'urt w'ere old Ishkabibble pushed it?"

Sanders shook his head.

"'Specs it does," said Hale judicially. "*I* know. An' 'e *may* be a Buckle, but 'e 'its like 'ell... Never mind, 'Oly, pull yerself tergevver! You gets all *wet*, that's wot's up wi' you. If we on'y had some rum I'd make yer blind. Do yer an 'elluva lot of good. Cheer yer up no end..."

Sanders looked up at him wearily. "Do you mind?" he said. "I would like to be alone."

Hale drove the cork into his water-bottle with an angry slap of his palm. His smile went, and a frown came to his forehead. "All *right*!" he said. "An' I 'opes a bloody great wolf'll come in the night an' slip it acrosst all yer rabbits... Surly sod! 'F yer thought more abaht yer measly self an' not so much abaht J. C., you'd be better off... An' so would 'E..." He turned and trudged off, the water-bottle dangling by its strap from his right hand.

He found the Sergeant sitting cross-legged away from the fire, now dying to a small heap of red embers.

"No need for this to-night, Hale." He looked up at the Cockney. "No broth for him… He's bad. Touch o' fever; probably sandfly."

"Ah." Hale dropped the bottle and sat, heavily. "Sandfly fever's a —!" He nodded towards the hut. "'E goin' to pull through?"

The Sergeant shrugged. "Hope so. But God alone knows, and He won't split… What can we do for him? … I had a little quinine, luckily… But that'll be gone in another dose…"

Hale looked into the ashes of the little fire. He said, without raising his head:

"Would it 'a been better 'f we'd of all gorn… not jest Jock an' the Matlow?"

The Sergeant dried the sweat from his palm against his breeches. He groped in his pocket and brought away a vast cigarette-case of leather; opened this and peered inside it. He counted twenty-three cigarettes. "Fag?" he said.

"Thank 'ee, Sarge." Hale put out a hand and caught the cigarette which was tossed to him. He plucked a glowing stick from the fire and in a moment was puffing.

The Sergeant took a deep breath of smoke and let it trickle, slow and voluptuous, from his nostrils. He said:

"We discussed all that, Hale. It wouldn't 've been possible for us all to go. There's Bell, for one thing… And another's the water… It's not mathematics, but though two men can come near to carrying enough water for two for say four days, eight can't take enough for eight for what'd be nearer a week… Anyway, I'm damn sure… an' I've been *thinking*… that what we've done's best."

Hale nodded. "Yes, Sawgint," he said. "'Course that's O.K... I was jest talkin', *as* per U... Sarge, are yer married?"

The Sergeant shook his head. "No. You?"

"Yeah... Been thinkin', I 'ave, as I wisht as 'ow I wasn't." He was talking now with his eyes turned groundwards. His hands rubbed gently at that aching back. "No grumbles, mindjer... nary one. We 'its off proper... But it's this war biz, that's wot gets me... They says: 'Fight, me boys! Fight for yer wife an' Chee-hildren!' That's all pukka; 'ot air, but some guts to it... But wot I wanta know *now*: wot the stinkin' 'ell's the good of gettin' pipped an' leavin' the old Trouble to fend for 'erself *an*' the boy? Eh?"

"But if everybody said that an' didn't go..." said the Sergeant.

Hale twisted uneasily. "I know... but it's all so ruddy *queer*, ain't it now? 'Chever line a bloke takes 'e's in the gyppo..." He broke off, leaving his sentence hung, as it were, on the still heavy air and the steady spiral column of the smoke from his cigarette, like mist in the moonlight.

"I was right jest now..." he said suddenly. "W'en I says I wan'ed a woman. Not 'arf I ruddy wasn't! 'Arf hour wi' that first bit I 'ad up Grant Road; that'd fix *me*... she was a classt A line... Ever get along Grant Road, Sarge, w'en we was over?"

"I know it," said the Sergeant. "But too much traffic to my mind... except the Jap houses, an' somehow you never got that feeling about them."

"I know wot yer *mean*," said Hale slowly. "Matter o' what a bloke likes... I'm not ejucated... wouldn't see things like you do... But that first one, she was Kelly's Eye... All the time I kep' thinkin': bloody queer to find 'er there... didn't seem to fit like... Funny colour she was, too: sorta cross atween coffee and lemon. Young, too! in Blighty you'd of put 'er down as eighteen... s'pose she was on'y abaht fourteen reely..." He broke off, to sit rapt a moment. The Sergeant smoked.

"Tell yer 'nother thing allus strikes me..." Hale looked up now, the memories fading from his eyes. "Queer 'ow folks looks at this goin' on the side... I wouldn't do it at 'ome, o' course... leastways not 'less driven to it... But right awye from Blighty... Gawd save us! does they think as 'ow a bloke c'n stay like a ruddy monk or wot? ... My ole girl don't spect it, that's one thing... she knows *me* ... But there *are* some as do. Not 'arf they don't an' all..."

He stopped suddenly. His head turned towards the hut beside him. Sounds came from the hut; muffled shoutings, murmurs, cries. The Sergeant leapt to his feet and disappeared within the doorway. The sounds continued a while; grew less; died away.

Hale, alone, changed his position. He lay flat on his back, hands locked behind his head. The pain in his back was worse; it spread now up to his shoulders and down to the sides of his knees... His head, too, was feeling strange; swollen and painful and light. His skin was burning and parched. He was not sweating tor the first time in many months.

The silence, utter and implacable and like a great weight on a man's chest, oppressed him and seemed actually to give him pain. He talked softly to himself through dry lips. "… — sandfly!" he said. "Little bahstuds gets under yer skin… fever… — it! … can't go sick *now*! … Stick it…" He groped for and found the water-bottle he had filled at the spring. He lay there, whispering to himself and at intervals taking draughts of the cool water. His head misbehaved itself.

The Sergeant came out of the hut. He opened the watch upon his wrist and peered at the faint, phosphorescent glowing of the hands and figures. He said:

"Hale! Time you an' I took over." He walked away from the hut and called: "Sanders! Sanders!" Through the trees the man came to him. "Take over again," said the Sergeant. "And watch out. He's bad. Very high temperature. I've given him quinine. There's a wet bandage on his head. Keep it wet; he seems to be quieter with it. Don't let him toss about 'case he opens that wound. Any difficulty wake Abelson or Morelli; they're comin' off guard now. 'F you *must*, send one o' them to fetch me. And, Sanders: no noise! Get me? Pray to yourself if you want to pray."

Sanders, rigidly at a travesty of attention, nodded his head. At a sign he turned and disappeared within the hut. The Sergeant went to the tree against which leaned his rifle. He said:

"Come on, Hale. Jildi. Got y'r rifle? I'll take the east side first. You go west and relieve Abelson. Patrol every now and then; not all the time."

Hale struggled to his feet. His rifle leaned against the wall of the hut; somewhere. A glint from a spear of moonlight piercing the tracery of the palm fronds showed him the barrel. He went to it and picked up the gun. It seemed of a weight almost unmanageable. His legs were unsteady. His head seemed vast and light, like a football. He said, in a thick squeak:

"Sawgint! I…" But he saw that the Sergeant had gone.

"Qui' ri',…" he muttered. "*Can't* go sick now… " He levered the rifle to his shoulder and walked, on legs momentarily steadier, through the trees.

Abelson came towards him, his neck held stiffly at that awkward angle. "'Bout time!" he muttered. "Nothin' doin' out there… Sweet Fanny! — hot, ain't it?" He walked away in the direction of the hut.

Hale drew deep breaths. He put a hand out and clutched for support at a palm trunk. He stood a moment, setting his teeth, then walked slowly and with leaden feet through the trees and to the edge of the knoll. He lay there, his rifle beside him. He propped that heavy head, that head which no longer felt like a football, but a pumpkin, on his hands and stared out across the moon-splashed waste with hot eyes, eyes which seemed fiery dents deep back in his skull.

Time passed him by. He lay there, now burning with a fire which seemed to be shrivelling the skin of his body as paper shrivels in flame, now shivering so that his lips trembled with sudden gusts of cold. But all the time he kept those fiery-feeling, aching eyes in a wide stare, looking out before him over the boundless semicircle of silver, black-dappled sand. At times his body seemed pressed hard against the hard, loose earth; at times it felt as though it had left that earth and was floating, ridiculously, in a bath of cold flame. At times his eyes would blur and specks of blue and red and green fire would dance about before them. But he rubbed at them, with a vicious hand which felt fat and flabby and ineffective, until the specks faded and went and once again he saw that black-splashed, shining sheet unroll itself in infinity. He spoke to himself, every now and then, sometimes from a mouth which seemed a cavern of flame, sometimes between teeth clenched firmly to prevent their chattering. He said:

"Can't go... *can't* go sick... Sick... Can't go sick! Gawd, if I c'd on'y *sweat!*"

It was immediately after one of those bouts when the specks danced before his eyes that he thought he saw something... a flicker of movement... away out there in the desert, straight in front of him... maybe four hundred yards, maybe a mile.

He rubbed at his eyes again, though they were clear. He thought: Mustn't get the willies! He waited.

Then he saw, again, just that same flicker of movement. How far away it might be he could not tell. It was as if the corner of one of those jagged shadows had uncoiled itself.

He waited... There! there it was again. Cautiously he got to his knees; his hand upon his rifle. The knees played him false. And his head. He fell over, limply, weakly. The world span about him. He lay upon his back and gritted his teeth. With an effort which left him shaking he got somehow to

123

his feet. He leaned, clutching in both hands his rifle, against the tree-trunk.

He saw the movement again, quite definite this time. He tried to raise the rifle to his shoulder, but failed. Now, striving to focus his eyes, he stared and saw more than movement. He saw a figure… or something black and upright where nothing black and upright had been. He giggled suddenly… like an excited girl. Strength in a measure returned to him.

"Can't see!" he muttered. "Can't see… get nearer… quite close… shoot ther…"

He walked on, stronger but yet wavering feet… for his head would not quite make up its mind what it wanted them to do. He came out of the shadow of the trees and plunged down the steep little slope and staggered on to the level floor of the desert.

He walked on, stolid and lurching… He stopped and knelt upon one knee and gazed… That black and upright something seemed clearer now, and bigger. "'Ave a poop at ther —!" he said.

He raised rifle to shoulder; but the barrel waved in eccentric curves. He bit at his lip until the blood came and trickled down over his chin. He held his breath. The barrel steadied; remained firm. He took careful aim… The black, upright thing appeared to move, very slightly… it became two black and upright things… He concentrated upon one of these…

His finger took the first pull of the trigger…

Then two blows struck him… two shocks, almost simultaneous and so terrific that he went backwards as if jerked by a lariat thrown from the back of a horse at full speed.

His rifle discharged itself into the sky. Even as the world went up in a great sheet of flaming darkness inside his head, he was conscious of a faint "phut-phut" and knew that the blows had been bullets…

He lay curiously twisted; the rifle, caught in some way between his body and his crumpled arm, pointed up to the sky like a finger. From him, as he lay, a thin and sluggish stream of darkness violated the shining sand.

XIV

THREE shots… a faint, double "phut" and a loud "crack" from close at hand…

The Sergeant, lying among the trees upon the eastern fringe, leapt to his feet and ran back and across the clearing. He came to the western side and threw himself flat and crawled until he was almost at the edge of the slope. He turned his head and softly called: "Hale!"

But before the word had properly left his lips his gaze had gone out over the desert, and he had seen. He rolled over upon his side and put a hand to his mouth. "Morelli!" he roared. "Abelson! Turn out! Turn out!" He twisted back again and brought the rifle to his shoulder. He could see nothing save sand and shadow and the crumpled body of Hale, the rifle beside pointing up into the sky.

But he fired. Three shots in the direction of that body and over it. They rang out with a noise which shattered the night. The sleeping men would hear *them* if they had not already heard his voice.

Abelson came, running, Morelli on his heels. "Get *down*!" said the Sergeant. "Crawl up level with me." They came, wriggling like great insects. Each had rifle and bandolier. Both were helmetless. Morelli wore shirt and breeches and socks; Abelson was the same but barefooted. "Whassup?" he said, in a sibilant shout intended for a whisper. "God!" Morelli said: his eyes had fallen upon that huddled body. "Look! you choot!" Abelson saw, and was quiet.

A rushing of feet and Sanders, fully dressed, was with them and lay panting at Morelli's side.

Then silence fell again about the four and the moon-drenched world.

"Can't see a — thing!" came Morelli's voice at last.

"Christ!" The Jew scrambled wildly to his feet.

"Down!" hissed the Sergeant. "*Down*, will you!" But Abelson still stood, his head bent forward, straining his eyes toward that limp mass which lay, black and huddled on the shining sand.

"He's movin'!" he gasped. "There! Look, I tell yeh! He's moved *twice*!" He flung out an arm, pointing with a hand which shook.

"Get *down*, damn you!" The Sergeant's voice rasped across the soft and heavy air. "They shot *him*, now they're waitin' for someone to go out for him. What chance 've y' got? Can't lose any more men…"

His voice ceased suddenly. For Abelson had dropped his rifle with a clattering crash. He seemed to gather himself, crouching as if for the start of a race. The Sergeant jerked to his knees and flung out a clutching hand. His fingers grazed a bare ankle but no more. For Abelson was already sliding down the slope, half running, half falling. They saw the flash of white feet as he reached the level and began to run.

"Bloody fool!" Morelli growled.

"Insubordinate swine!" The Sergeant brought his rifle back to his shoulder. "Guts, though… Now *watch*, all of you… Watch like all hell! Over there, beyond Hale. 'F you see anything, fire and go on firing…"

They looked out, holding their breath as if this would put those extra yards into their sight. They were, though their eyes were out beyond, conscious all the while of the racing, crouching figure of Abelson, covering those hundred and fifty yards of loose, deep, shifting dust like a sullen streak... They knew when he reached his goal and dropped on his knees beside it and bent over it with fevered urgency...

A shout from Morelli: "There! There!"... A string of shots, splitting the night... the Sergeant kneeling now, rifle still at shoulder, peering... Morelli re-loading, saying: "— it! Out there... two fingers right of the square shadder two hundred past the guys. For Jesus' sake shoot, you —s!"... More shots... a crescendo of emptying magazines, Morelli's and the Sergeant's... Stray, queerly vague-sounding shots from Sanders... The Jew, bending, straining out there, a black ape in the silver light, to get upon his shoulders the limp bundle... He does it; and rises, to bend again and somehow snatch and grasp the bundle's fallen rifle... He comes labouring back, trotting clumsily on wavering feet, bowed beneath his burden...

Firing at that patch which Morelli had seen, or thought to see, as something more than shadow... Was it? ... Two spurts... three... four... of sand about the feet of the Jew and his bundle... No sound, for the rifles cracking in their ears drown those others whose bullets had made the sand-spray... But they see them... Loading with oaths and speed... pulling triggers so fast as fingers will work; Morelli and the Sergeant... Slower, vaguer shots from Sanders... A hail of bullets... a screen of them, screaming out to that place where the shadow had seemed more than shadow…

There were no more spurts of sand. Abelson reached the slope, toiled up it with one last effort, and rolled among them. His burden fell from him and lay sprawled at the feet of Sanders while he himself doubled up and strove for breath with raucous, whistling gasps.

"Cease fire!" The Sergeant rose from his knee. "Morelli: keep watching." He laid down his rifle and ran to the body of Hale. He knelt beside it and groped with his hand in the bosom of its shirt, bending his head, too, its ear to the mouth.

"I think," he said. "Yes… Finish."

Abelson, from the ground, gasped denial. "Not on yeh life! … Wasn't out there… Spoke."

There came a faint twitching in the body under the Sergeant's hands. He bent his head again sharply. Through the darkness, striking his ear so faintly that it was as if a voice spoke inside his own head, came the words:

"Good ole Neb… Neb… Nebu'k'neezer! … Wot O! ther King o' th' Jews!" A pause. Then: "Good boy… pullin' us aht o' that… Got… to… go… sick now…" The voice went out like a snuffled candle. Silence. Then a choking, bubbling gasp. A rattling, yet liquid sound. The body, which had seemed to swell as the words had come from its head, went limp and utterly still.

The Sergeant got to his feet. "Gone now," he said. He stood for a moment looking down, through the darkness at the shadow, at the darker mass at his feet. "Pity," he said.

Abelson, his breath still coming in rasping gasps, came and stood at his elbow. "Wha's that?" he said. He looked down at the body.

"Out," said the Sergeant.

Abelson knelt and ran his hand under the shirt. He rose again. "— it!" he said. "— *it!*" He turned away.

"Get y'r rifle," came the Sergeant's voice after him. "You an' Morelli keep *watching*. Mallam?" He turned. "Sanders!" he said. "Get back to the hut." He walked away among the trees, making for the spring.

By it, propped against a tree, he found what he sought, two water-bottles. He filled them and turned back on the way he had come.

He stood over Morelli and Abelson. "Pawney?" he said. A yard to his left lay the body of Hale, still and limp.

Morelli said, without taking his eyes from the desert, "Thank 'ee, Sarge."

The Sergeant bent, but straightened suddenly and with a jerk. Among the trees, coming towards them, were running, stumbling, crazy footsteps. Sanders burst upon them. "Corporal…" he panted. "Corporal… Corporal's… Corporal's…"

The Sergeant put down the bottles. "Stay here," he said to the men on the ground. "Sanders!" He picked up his rifle and went to the man and gripped the thin arm. His fingers sunk into the flesh. "What's up?" he said. He drew the man back over the way he had come at that stumbling run.

"Corporal Bell…" panted Sanders. "He's…" The Sergeant dropped the arm and began to run. He came out into the clearing and cut across its edge, towards the hut. He made at full speed for that doorway.

But he did not go through it. Across the threshold, outside, lay Bell. His legs were doubled beneath him, and by his head a rifle lay in the dust. He was clothed, fully, even to the topee. His bandolier was across his chest. He lay in a patch of moonlight, which gave the effect, incredibly realistic, of the pool made by a lime from the gallery.

The Sergeant halted. He stood, leaning on his rifle, looking down at the body. He had seen, it had been shown to him with a clarity utterly brutal… He knew that this was a dead man. Another dead man.

"My *God*!" he muttered.

Sanders came, and laid a hand upon his arm. He said: "Sergeant, is he…"

The Sergeant nodded. "Poor devil… Must 've heard that firin'… through his fever 'n all… Got up… dressed… tried to come out. Couldn't really 've known what he was at. Instinct. Then that wound tore open. Bled to death, if the cropper he came didn't do the job outright."

Sanders' hand fell to his side. His knees seemed to give. He sank upon them and bowed his head upon his hands. He began to pray.

"O Father…" His voice cracked. Sobs tore at him, racked his thin body.

XV

NOON... the sun, for the third time since that day whose night had seen the death of Hale and then the Corporal, beat vertically down upon the oasis and its garrison... Save for Morelli, upright upon the roof of the hut, shading his eyes to look out over the desert, there was no sign of life.

Inside the hut, naked to the waist, the sweat from their bodies making dark, spreading patches upon the blankets folded beneath them, lay the Sergeant and Abelson. They had found that, oven though it was, so that a man seemed slowly and helplessly to roast within it, the hut was the place in which to find not indeed comfort but a lesser torture during those hours between eight and eight.

The Sergeant raised himself upon a brown and corded arm. He groped in his haversack and brought from it a piece of rag which had once been a handkerchief. He mopped with this; at his neck, which felt slimy to his touch as if it had been bathed in oil; at his chest, down which ran little rivulets as he moved; at his arms and back, on which, in unreachable spots, the sweat, as it will on backs when men recline in great heat, lay in cold and gruesome patches.

He threw the limp, drenched rag away to rest upon his haversack. He said:

"Where's Sanders?" in a voice which was flat and stale and tired.

Abelson grunted. "Yeh knows as much as I do. I c'n guess, though..."

"H'm…" The Sergeant nodded. "Took his haversack, didn't he? Can't see it. What's that for?" His voice was that of a man who talks for the sake of smashing silence. The Jew grunted again and closed his eyes, puffing his breath out audibly through his lips with every exhalation.

The Sergeant struggled into his shirt of khaki flannel, pulling viciously to get the damp stuff over his damper body. He buckled on his spine-pad and clapped upon his head his topee. From where it leaned in a corner he took his rifle, hitched it into the crook of his left arm, and stepped out through the doorway… from oven to furnace.

He looked up at Morelli. "All clear?" he said.

Morelli looked down at him. "As U!" he said. "What's the budgi, Sarge? It's like all hell up here!" He panted a little as he spoke. For an instant he seemed to sway as if falling, but recovered.

The Sergeant looked at his watch. "'Nother quarter 'f an hour. Stick it!" He turned back to doorway again. "Abelson!" he called, and received a grunt for answer. "Morelli's hour's nearly up. You go on in fifteen minutes. Better get ready." He turned away and walked through the trees to the edge of the clearing and across it.

He came to the spring and stopped to drink from the palm of his hand and to lave face and neck. He passed on into the trees behind the spring: these were denser here than elsewhere and had more undergrowth and young trees about their feet.

Before he came within sight of Sanders, the man's voice, on that high and piercing note, came to his ears.

"'Now if Christ be preached that he rose from the dead, how say some among you that there is no resurrection of the dead? But if there be no resurrection of the dead, then is Christ not risen: And if Christ be not risen, then is our preaching vain, and your faith is also vain.'..."

The Sergeant brushed through the undergrowth and passed close between two trunks and saw. Sanders knelt beside a long narrow mound. His hands held close before his face a small book whose khaki cover bore a cross of red. The Sergeant's footsteps roused him. He shut the little Bible and got to his feet and turned. Beneath the shading helmet his face was brown-grey with eyes which stared, blazing, out from under a harassed brow. The flesh of his face seemed to have fallen away so that only skin was left, and this so tightly stretched that the high, slanting cheek-bones looked as if they would at any moment push their way out from beneath it. He stood rigidly, awkwardly, in that unconscious travesty of attention. His hands, clenched at his sides, one holding the Bible, were trembling.

The Sergeant looked at him, then down at the mound which marked the grave of Bell and Hale. He remembered how, on that night three night ago, they had laboured over that grave, sweating in the moonlight. Two at a time they had worked, two digging, two, at the far side of the oasis, on guard. He and Sanders had actually finished the grave; it was they who had put in the bodies and piled down the earth and made the mound. He remembered how, at last, he had left Sanders there, praying. He saw that, since the day before, someone... Sanders... had made from palm leaves a large, rough cross which now stood, leaning drunkenly, at one end of the mound. He said, after this moment's silence:

"How long you been here?"

The thin lips moved in that ravaged face. Their words were spoken so low that the Sergeant thrust forward his head to catch them. "Almost an hour, Sergeant."

The Sergeant looked up at the sun, which streamed down on to the grave unhindered at this spot by palms which might break its force. "You better get inside," he said curtly. "Quick. An' don't do this again. You've got your relief to do on the roof, an' that's enough sun for any man. Come here at night… if you must. Take my advice, you won't… Look here, Sanders… whatever you were, or are goin' to be, just get it into your head that *now* you're a soldier. As a soldier you've got to do, while we're here, what I think's best… And what's best now is to take y'r turns at guard an' look out *and* take care of y'rself… See? That's our job now, keeping as fit's we *can*… in case of whatever's comin'… Understand?"

"Yes," said the pale lips, wet now with the beads of sweat which suddenly were rolling from the cheeks and forehead.

The Sergeant came closer. He put out a hand and rested it a moment on the thin shoulder. "Remember it, then," he said. "You want to watch yourself, Sanders…" His voice changed; became curt again. "Now get back. Lie down. An' try an' sleep until your relief. You've got two hours. Abelson goes on now; then me; then you. Get along."

Sanders went. The Sergeant stood and watched until the awkward, thin figure was lost to sight among the trees.

He scratched his head, then shook it. He said, half-aloud: "Go *right* off... any day... nearly is now... An' that's that... Who wouldn't be a soldier; a dashin' slashin' cavalry soldier!" He turned from the grave and made his way slowly to the spring. He sat down, heavily, in the shade at the base of a palm. He brought out that leather case and counted the cigarettes inside it. There were twelve. He hesitated over these a moment; finally took one and lighted it and leaned back luxurious against the tree, tilting his helmet forward over his eyes. He thought. He had been thinking, in these ever-recurring circles, since that night... how long ago was it? ... when Cook and MacKay had trudged off, walking and walking until they had walked themselves away. Four nights ago! That was it... seemed longer... No, by God! it was *three* only... the same night that Hale had died, and Bell... What a night? Thinking in circles, he'd been... Ever since then. Damn it! You couldn't *help* thinking round and round... it was like a mouse in a cage, working one of those treadmills... There was no other way you could think... It *was* a circle... Oasis... Cook and MacKay and their search for aid... No knowledge of where they were or we are or the whole blasted British Army either... Stay or go... Can't go... not enough grub left now except dates... don't know where to go to... If go, might miss troops sent by Jock and Cook if they'd got anywhere... Not many Arabs holdin' us up here; can't be, or they'd 've been all over us... Wait, then... Watch... water, dates, live... Oasis... The circle complete.

The smoke from his cigarette curled lazily up into the burning, shimmering air. The sweat, where he leaned his back against the tree, grew cold and clammy. But he sat there. He smoked. His mind once more started upon its treadmill.

In the hut lay Sanders and Morelli, for now it was Abelson who stood upon the roof above them... Morelli was naked to the waist: he lay flat upon his back, his arms outflung; his broad, thick torso rose and fell in great jerks to his laboured breathing. Sanders was in shirt and breeches; he had cast off merely helmet, spine-pad, and bandolier. He lay upon his stomach, his hands propping his chin: open before him was the little Bible. There was silence save for the gasps of Morelli and the faint, faint mutter which rose, every now and then, from the grey lips that moved perpetually as the eyes above them read on through the Book of Revelation.

The Sergeant came. He put his rifle in the corner and threw down his helmet. He sat cross-legged, upon his blankets. He said:

"Just a minute, Sanders! You awake, Morelli?" They turned their faces towards him. "Want to tell you," he said: "there's one tin o' beef left. And ten biscuits. We've got to start livin' on dates. Quarter of the bully for each man to-night, and half a biscuit... and dates. To-morrow biscuit an' dates... Day after, dates an' biscuit... Then dates, boos. Thought I'd let you know." He uncoiled his legs and lay down, propping himself upon an elbow. "Tobacco," he said. "What about it? Been thinkin'. Rather rely on your own stock, or pool it all with me an' I'll ration it?"

"There'd be only three in that," Morelli said. He jerked a thumb towards Sanders' corner. "He don't indulge... do yer, Padre? ... You, I mean, Sanders!"

"Did you want me?" Sanders lifted pale glowing eyes in mild interrogation.

Morelli fell back upon his blankets. "Oh *no*!" he said. "But you do not, I think, indulge in the disreptable vice of the noxious weed Nickertina?"

"No," said Sanders, "I do not smoke." His tone was aloof and absent. His eyes, before these few words had left his mouth, were strayed back to the small, muddy print of his Bible.

"Gawd A'mighty!" Morelli said. "Thank *you*, Bishop! Nor you don't drink, I s'pose. Nor never have a woman... Yore too bloody pure to be true, that's what, your Holiness... Sit there, all the — time... Read, read, read... Pray, pray, pray... Read, pray, read! Pickin' out the juicy bits, I'll bet... an' from what *I* can remember, which ain't much, there's more'n a few o' them... Sarge! betcha ten rupees he gets all shivery ev'ry time he finds 'harlot.' Ur..."

The Sergeant sat up. "Chubbarow, Morelli," he said. "Leave the man alone." His voice was not tired now: it cut across the stagnant, fiery air like a whip-lash. "What's come over you? Not like you. Shut up!"

A dark, slow flush deepened the tan of Morelli's square, blunt face. "Sorry!" he mumbled. "Sorry, Sergeant... Bit jumpy like, I am... You was talkin' about baccy. I got four blood-spitters an' 'bout a half-ounce o' twist... The Yid's got 'bout thirteen-fourteen fags."

"We're about square, then." The Sergeant lay down again, hands locked behind his neck. "No good rationing... I'm goin' to sleep."

While Sanders read his Bible and Morelli lay panting and scowling up at the roof above them, he slept, for half an hour. He woke upon the tick of that half-hour. He left the hut and called down Abelson and took his place upon the roof. Nothing, said the Jew, had happened or moved or smelt; there was... just — sand.

Abelson entered the hut. He flung down his topee with a crash. He tore off his shirt. He collapsed upon his blankets and was silent for perhaps ten minutes, while Morelli scowled up at the roof and Sanders read his Bible.

He sat up suddenly, after those few minutes. His dark and sullen face was bright with the sweat upon it. His full red mouth was twisted into its snarling grin. Every now and then his hand crept up to the side of his neck and massaged it with tender fingers. He said:

"Nice cheery lot o' bahstuds!"

Morelli lay, still scowling up. Sanders, his lips moving in their ceaseless, soundless mumble, read on. Abelson surveyed them.

"*I don't* think!" he said. Then: "Wake *up*! Wake *up*! you dung-headed soors! God stiffen me, you'll drive me up the — pole. Lyin' about there!"

Morelli said, his eyes still frowning at the roof, "Put a bag in it! Make more row'n a Band of Hope outin'."

"—!" said Abelson. He got to his feet and crossed to where Sanders lay, and knelt beside him. "What you readin', Soapy?" he said. He put out a hand and twitched the book away.

"Leave 'im *alone!*" Morelli said.

The Jew laughed. "Not goin' to hurt the silly bleeder! What's this? Holy Bible. Holy —! … Aah! Would you, then! Naughty naughty!" He thrust out an arm and pinned the writhing Sanders to his blankets. "Stay still, teddima-choot!" he said, and laughed.

Sanders under that heavy arm, grew suddenly still as death. But his body was rigid, every muscle in it tense.

"Leave the guy *alone!*" Morelli said from his blankets. But he spoke wearily, like an old man to children, automatically sounding reproof with no hope of having obedience paid to his orders and neither the intention nor the means of enforcing them.

"Oh, chubbarow!" Abelson's tone was contemptuous. He suddenly swung a leg across Sanders' body and sat, heavily, upon the thin and narrow back. He took the Bible in both hands and opened it at random. With every movement the sweat broke out upon his white torso, so that it glistened, gleaming, in the dull, quiet light of the hut. He began to read, in a high, nasal, giggling whine:

"'Notwithstanding I have a few things against thee, because thou sufferest that woman Jez-jezeebel, which calleth herself a prophetess to teach and seduce my servants to commit fornication and to eat things sacrificed unto idols. And I gave her space to repent of her fornication, and she repented not. Behold I will cast her into a bed…'"

Morelli sat up; rose to his knees; stood. He suddenly shouted: "Close that stinkin' mouth o' yours, you sod of a bleedin' Kosher!"

In a bound Abelson too was on his feet. Then, behind him, Sanders.

The Jew stood facing Morelli. He whispered with a hissing sound that seemed louder than a cry: "What did yeh say! … Just say it again… I wanta make sure…"

On the heels of his words came words from Sanders behind him; a high-pitched cry, hysteric:

"You should have read on! What does it say! 'I will give unto every one of you according to your works.'"

They ignored him. For them, at that moment, Sanders did not exist. Morelli, his naked chest shaken with those stuttering gasps which tell of nerves stretched to breaking-point, came nearer. He shouted, across the high wild tones of Sanders:

"I said: 'Chubbarow, you udder-faced — of a bloody Kosher!' D'yer hear *now*? You stinkin' Jew!" He came closer still, so that now he stood within a foot of Abelson and was forced to look up into the dark, scowling face above him.

"Right!" said Abelson. He took a step back. His hands dropped to his belt and drew it tighter about him. "Right, Mr. Houdini-or-whatever-yer-Dago-name-may-be! I'll shove them words back down y'r bleeding throat along with all them pretty teeth. Yeh…"

Sanders' voice again. "'… unto every one of you according to your works…'"

Then silence. Abelson stepped back farther. His hands became fists, his arms inexorable pistons, the oil upon them glistening as gently they slithered in and out. His scowl gave way to the fighting snarl, half contemptuous leer.

Morelli stood thick and short and square. Strong but hopeless. His hands, too, became fists, but awkward lumps, with the arms above them just arms. He shook with rage. He shouted:

"Come *on*, then!"

Abelson's feet became light and dancing feet. He moved nearer…

There was a rushing, sliding rumble above their heads and the sound of a fall. The Sergeant came in upon them like a savage gale. He caught Morelli by a shoulder, with fingers which cut into the flesh, and sent him reeling, to come with a thud against the wall and slide down in an unbalanced heap to the floor. He put the flat of his hands against the naked breast of Abelson and thrust him, all his weight behind the thrust, to fall headlong upon Sanders' blankets. He caught Sanders by the neck-band of his sodden shirt and swung him round and sent him crashing down upon the sprawling body of the Jew.

He stood in the centre and glared round upon them. His helmet was pushed back from his forehead. His face, dark with tan and black with the anger upon it, seemed to jut out from beneath the helmet's brim like a beast from the

The Sergeant came in upon them like a savage gale.

opening to its lair. He crouched a little, his shoulders thrust forward, his arms bent, the hands upon them open, with crooked fingers.

"You festering swine!" he said. "You blasted pack of Sunday School soldiers! Squabblin' an' blindin' an' prayin' an' trying to start y'r damn-fool little scraps! What the flaring hell d'you think you *are*? And, by God, what d'you take *me* for! Just because I let Cook give Abelson a tanning for everyone's sake, d'you think I'm goin' to put up with *this* sort o' thing. By God! you're *meant* to be soldiers. And I'll *make* you soldiers, you bloody fools! ... Morelli! get on your shirt an' kit an' get up on that roof. *Quick*! An' stay there till you're relieved. Sanders! give him a back up. An' get out yourself among the trees and watch too! *Move*, will you! Drop that damn' book! Abelson! get up! Get on y'r kit an' go out, *now*, and start bangin' down some dates. An go on until *I* tell you to stop."

Abelson, his dark eyes smouldering, got slowly to his feet. Morelli, quietly docile, scrambled into his shirt. Sanders lay where Abelson's rising had thrust him.

The Sergeant kept his position; tense, ready, it seemed, to spring. His eyes swung round to the sprawling Sanders.

"Quick, you!" he said. His gaze came back to Abelson, whose fists once again were working, whose lips, saliva white at their twisted corners were saying:

"Knock us about, would yeh? ..."

The Sergeant's body straightened. He laughed. A strange, fierce sound. He said:

"You're not just a fool, my lad. You're *silly*, that's what … What you goin' to do, d'you think? Hit me? … You fool kid! You an' your twopenny-ha'penny scrapping! If we were out o' this, I'd take you on… rough-house, mark you… I'd let you know what a *men's* scrap is! I was rough-housin' my way about the world, Abelson, before your mother 'd finished sucklin' you… But that's enough… Do as I've told you, *now*!" His hand flashed to his pocket and came away with the subaltern's automatic, wicked and squat and blue, in his fingers. "I'm in charge here," he said. His eyes met the eyes of the Jew, which dropped. "Jildi!" he said…

They went, with speed and in silence, to their allotted tasks. The Sergeant, alone, thrust the pistol into his pocket. He sat, cross-legged, upon Morelli's blankets.

He threw down his helmet and wiped with sticky arm at his streaming forehead. He took out his case and from it a cigarette.

He sat, placidly smoking. As he smoked, a slow, quiet smile twisted his mouth. He began to blow rings, one through another. The smoke wreathed itself in a blue haze about his head.

XVI

SANDERS came out of the hut into the moonlight which filtered through the palms. Behind him, inside, Morelli slept quiet and Abelson with much tossing and moaning and hard, raucous breathing.

Sanders, after a moment's pause, turned and trudged off through the trees. The helmet, the bandolier, the rifle—all, in fact, of his military trappings, seemed upon him utterly incongruous.

He plunged in among the trees of the western side, and came presently upon a man who lay, rifle before him, gazing out over the desert. He looked down at the man. He said: "It's time, Sergeant."

The Sergeant looked at his watch, then rose to his feet, hooking his rifle by its sling to his shoulder. "Quite right," he said. "That hour an' a half soon goes… Keep your eyes peeled, now, Sanders. There's been nothing yet. I'll see Morelli relieves you at the proper time." He turned to go, but was stopped by an urgent voice and a hand laid upon his arm.

"Sergeant!" said Sanders, in a voice hoarse and many tones lower than its habit. "Sergeant! Is it four days since MacKay left us? And Cook?"

The Sergeant nodded. "That's what I make it… No; it's three. Four to-morrow night. Why?"

"I was wondering…" Sanders began. The voice was now so low that the Sergeant was forced to bend his head to catch it. "I thought… I mean, if they have been… successful… If they have… got through, should not they be… be here

146

soon, with us… bringing people to fetch us? Do you think so, Sergeant… Do you?" His hand upon the Sergeant's arm had tightened its grip; the long fingers seemed to possess a strength quite disproportionate.

The Sergeant shook free his arm. He looked down at the man's averted face, half irradiated by a splash of moonlight, half obscured by the black shadow of the helmet-brim. He said:

"Couldn't say. No, I don't think they could 've done more yet than join up with some of our folk… That means another day or so for any troops to get back along here."

Sanders turned his head so that now his whole face seemed, in the light, to leap into being. "It was only…" he said, whispering, "only that I had a dream… Last night… I did not sleep well… less, I think, than an hour… But I dreamed that they had come back… That is all I knew before I waked; that they had returned…" Here his gaunt, strained face with its wild look and burning eyes was distorted by a sudden smile, so unexpected as to come with the shock of a blow. "So you see," he said, "that all will be well." There came from his long, lean throat a sound which passed for laughter.

The Sergeant said curtly:

"Dessay! Now get on with y'r job." He turned on his heel and walked away among the trees. He halted once and stepped behind a tree and peered back in the direction from whence he had come. His eyes, straining, could just make out the form of Sanders, lying where he himself had lain, with head lifted the better so see out over the wastes of gleaming sand.

After that reassuring glance, he went on his way towards the hut. He bore in his mind the picture of that sudden, rather dreadful smile, and in his ears that lifeless laugh, more distressing in its travesty of coyness than in its hint of incipient insanity. He walked with head bent in thought. He knew, by the time he reached the hut, that this night must be the last on which, for even an hour, Sanders should be the guard. To-night would do; but not again… He entered the hut and found his blankets and cast himself quietly down upon them. He pondered over this small new difficulty… There would be only three of 'em for guards now… Sanders would idle about, praying, getting madder and madder… He'd have to be found jobs… But what jobs? … The little hitch swelled and swelled in his mind until it seemed a problem which filled the world and bore down upon him intolerably…

He sat up abruptly. He cursed himself in silence. "Shut up, you!" he thought… "You're as bad as he is!"… He bullied himself, at last, into an orderly frame of mind and sank back upon the blankets again and closed his eyes.

Despite the choking gasps and snores of the restless Abelson which vilely assaulted the darkness, he felt himself, at last, drifting towards peace… his body and mind were wrapped in that soft, delicious cloak which is the first wave of sleep.

Then, with a brutal suddenness, this cloak was torn from him. There was a movement in the dark, a rustling.

Then Morelli's voice, saying, with that thick clarity common to the voices of men who speak while asleep:

"Ten little Nigger Boys!" Silence. Then: "That's *it*! Ten! An' then they was None!" Another silence. Then a low, thick chuckling.

Abelson waked. There was more rustling as he too sat up. "What the *hell*?" he said savagely. "*Shert* up, you!"

"*And* you!" The Sergeant's voice went wearily through the darkness.

Morelli, still sleeping, mumbled inarticulately; fell silent; slumped back to lie again.

The hut grew quiet.

Out among the trees Sanders lay where the Sergeant had left him. But his eyes were not searching the desert. They were closed, tightly screwed-up like a child's, behind the hands which covered his face. He was speaking, a broken breathless mumble. "… beseech Thee, O Lord, to deliver this, the humblest of Thy mighty host of servants, from the thing which weighs him down…

"O God! Help me! Christ! Lift from me this shrouding thing! Jesus, Thou didst not fear when they cried out from the body of the hall: 'Crucify Him! Crucify Him!' Thou didst not fear when they led Thee out from there and put the Cross upon Thy back; Thou didst not fear even when the moment of Thine agony had come…

"O Lamb of God! O Saviour! O Lion of the Tribe of Judah! Pity me, for I am afraid! Hear me, *hear me*! I am afraid, afraid, *afraid*!"

The mumble rose to a muffled cry.

"… afraid! Is *this* my punishment? Jesu! I implore Thee… if I may not be granted peace from this hell of fear, send me Sleep. Dear God, send me *Sleep*! …"

The voice died away. The man lay, trembling, his hands yet pressed tightly to his face.

He whispered in his throat: "*Hear me! Hear me!* Jesus whom I adore!"

There came, it seemed to him, a sweet and gentle answer to his prayer. For a great aching peace stole through him, so that his taut and trembling body relaxed into ecstatic softness… No more were there reeling through his head those voiceless, nameless fears which had beset him: no more did the trees about him shelter vague, disastrous forms unseen and unheard but felt with every cringing nerve: no more was the silence filled with rustlings and whispers and scheming, guttural, loathsome voices which spoke in strange uncouth tongue of how pain and death should come to him… pain, pain, and pain before that death.

No more did pictures rise behind his eyelids of these others; of Pearson and Brown, of Hale, of the Corporal as he had lain dead, with the moonlight on his face, across the threshold of the hut, the blood from his opened wound spreading dark over the silvered earth. At last and after many days, fear had left him. He was pure and cool and free. He was light, light. And now would follow, when the next man had come to take his place, long, unhurried, swelling Sleep…

The hands fell limp away from his face. They lay before him, pale in the filtered moonlight. He gazed at them. His eyelids closed. His head fell forward upon those hands and the rifle-barrel beside them. He slept.

And away before him, out on the desert, something moved. A long darkness, thicker than the shadow from which it had emerged, crawled with slow but unceasing movement towards the oasis. At every hundred yards or so this movement ceased; as if the mover were waiting the answer to its movement.

But answer there was none. Among the trees, Sanders slept, a great peace upon that strange, gaunt face. And the movement went on.

It drew close and closer, this thick, creeping shadow. So close that had the eyes of Sanders been opened they would have seen that behind the thick blackness trailed, jerkily, comically, a thicker more clumsy whiteness, shining in the moon rays.

The movement ceased. Now, there were not more than ten yards separating it from the beginning of the slope to the trees. It ceased for minutes together; then, cautiously, began again. But not the same movement.

Upon his hands, the head of Sanders stirred. Then was still. Then stirred again and was lifted.

He waked, at once and completely. There had rushed into his mind, from somewhere, the memory that his eyes were needed.

He saw, at the foot of the slope, two white blurs and a thick, black shadow which was no shadow. On the instant he was filled again with those clamant leprous fears.

Shaking, he somehow got his rifle to his shoulder. He fired, wildly, emptying his magazine. The thick black shadow straightened. It became the figure of a man, in dark robes, which turned and ran, its kaftan flying in a wild stream behind its head. It ran, not straight, but in a regular zig-zag, ever lengthening.

Sanders fumbled with shaking hand at a pouch of his bandolier. His magazine needed another clip. The button of the pouch seemed fast wedged…

Morelli, when those shots had been fired, was dressing himself for his coming relief. The sharp crackle of the rifle smote on his ears. He was on his feet in a bound. "*Turn out!*" he bellowed and snatched his rifle. He shot from the hut and raced through the trees. He came to the western fringe and hurled himself flat and raked the desert with his eyes. He saw the running, dodging figure, now half-way back to those bars of black shadow from which it had come.

His rifle came to his shoulder. Its barrel followed steadily the sweeps and darts of that diminishing figure.

"Sod 'im!" he muttered. He aimed, carefully, a few feet to the right of that darting figure. He fired. "Wow!" he cried. "Got the bleeder!" For the figure had lurched, spun round, and fallen. It lay like a stain upon the sand.

With a thudding of boots came the Sergeant and "Abelson, both stripped to the waist but carrying rifles and with laden bandoliers ludicrous across their naked chests.

The Sergeant lay beside Morelli. Abelson dropped, too, but farther to the right, between Morelli and the invisible Sanders.

"What's on?" the Sergeant said. He looked. He saw that dark blot two hundred yards away. "Good!" he said. "Any more of 'em?"

"Not seen any," Morelli grunted. "How'd this start, anyway?"

From their right came the crackle of Sanders' rifle. At last his fumbling, shaking fingers had reloaded. He fired now utterly at random…

"What the *hell*?" The Sergeant leapt to his feet and raced through the trees. He came upon Sanders just as the second clip was spent. He dropped down beside the man and laid a hand on the wavering rifle. "What you at?" he said. "Where are they?"

Sanders turned to him a face which made him start. The man's helmet had fallen off and there was no shadow to hide from the moon-ray, coming down between the tree-tops, those half-closed eyes, those open, loose lips, saliva flecking their corners, that whole semblance of semi-idiotic terror.

The Sergeant looked away. "What happened first?" He spoke sharply.

There came no reply, and he did not wait for one. For his eyes had fallen upon those two whitenesses lying below him at the foot of the slope. He drew in his breath with a sharp hiss. He got to his feet and went nearer, right to the edge, and looked down.

"Almighty God!" he said between his teeth. He lifted his voice. "Morelli! Abelson!" he called.

They came running. He stood, pointing. Their eyes followed his arm. They gasped.

"It's Englishmen!" Morelli whispered.

Abelson craned forward. Suddenly he laughed, a high note of hysteria. "You bloody fool!" he cried, "it's Jock an' the Matlow! …"

Silence fell upon them, aching silence. The Sergeant said, at last:

"They can't be left there… like that."

"We'll get 'em. Him an' me." Abelson jerked a thumb towards Morelli.

"No!" said the Sergeant. "One's enough. You an' Morelli lie here. 'F you see a movement out there, start shootin' like all hell. I shan't be much of a mark. An' it'll only take half a minute."

He threw off his bandolier and plunged down the slope. His naked torso must have made a shining target at once discernible, for there came two distinct reports and spurts of sand, one at his feet, the other short of him by two yards. Above him, Abelson and Morelli opened fire with a burst so rapid as to sound almost like that of a Vickers gun…

The Sergeant stooped and caught in either hand a cold, stiff, white arm, one thin and sinewy, the other enormous with lumps of knotted muscle like twisted cables… He turned away his eyes, for what he had seen had made his gorge to rise and almost choke him… He backed, bent double and hauling, up the slope.

Over his head Abelson and Morelli kept up their hail of bullets. But two more shots came from the shadows, one so close that the sand it sprayed splashed, stinging, upon the Sergeant's face. He strained, panting, racking every muscle. He got his double burden of twenty-two odd stone at last to the crest and over it and into the shadow.

He lay, panting, some feet away from the two white things which he had dragged. Morelli and Abelson ceased firing. They twisted their heads to look.

"Oh my *Christ*!" mumbled Abelson.

Morelli was silent, but lurched suddenly to his feet and took three steps away and began to vomit.

Sanders, like a thin ghost, came from where he lay. He stood looking down at the two bodies as they rested in that pool of moonlight which somehow gave their utter nakedness a kind of extra horror. There was no scar upon those bodies save the mark of the rope which had dragged them back to their fellows… this mark and that one most shameful mutilation.

Sanders said, softly and with a strange suddenness:

"Their faces… how… what are those? …" Then: "Oh!" he shrieked suddenly on the dreadful head note of a woman's scream. "Oh! … No. No. *No!*" His rifle dropped with a clatter at his feet. He flung an arm across his eyes and turned and fled wildly back through the trees.

XVII

Let him go!" the Sergeant said; for Abelson had started forward. "Get those entrenchin' tools. Jildi!"

The Jew went, running. Morelli, recovered, stood clear of the trunk against which he had leant. He stooped and picked up his fallen rifle; in the moonlight which pierced the shadow where it lay, his face showed pallidly green.

The Sergeant went to him. "You get down here," he said. "An' watch out. Abelson and I'll get the other job done right away."

Morelli got down. He muttered thickly:

"Thought I *had* a cast-iron belly! But *that's* got me all right all right! ... Never puked before, not even when that 18-pounder dropped a couple right into B Squadron at Eisal 'fore we knew it was there... an' that *was* a mess, if you like! ... But *that*!" He jerked his head behind him and shivered.

The Sergeant nodded. "Makes it worse, too, when you know the fellers. I've seen it before... once. Bad enough then... but with Jock and Cook..."

He broke off as Abelson returned, panting, with the little spades. He went to meet him and took one of these. He looked about him, measuring with his eye certain spaces. "Just there'll do," he said. "Come on. Let's get at it. Morelli's watchin' out there."

Abelson threw from him his bandolier. Half-naked, sweating until a little rain ran from their bodies to splash upon the earth, they toiled in silence for half an hour or more.

Abelson straightened himself for a moment, hands pressed to his aching back. "God!" he muttered. "God! … The bloody — sons of —!" He bent again to the task. But now, as he worked, he talked.

"Sergeant!" he said. "What they do that *for*? What the *hell*! Shoot 'em all neat like that… no mess… through the back o' the head… Why not leave 'em… Why do *that*? …"

The Sergeant grunted. "Why everythin'? … It's an old trick of the Arab women…"

"Women!" cried the Jew. "Women! 'F I caught the bitch that done *that* I'd…" He said what he would do.

"But this mayn't 've been women," the Sergeant said. "Don't see how…" He broke off and stepped out of the pit they had dug. "That's deep enough," he said.

Abelson climbed out and stood by his side. They both had their backs to that place where lay the bodies of Cook and MacKay. They were conscious of those bodies, and of extreme reluctance again to look upon them. They stood awkwardly, saying nothing, yet most acutely aware that delay must end and the time come when with their hands they must put those white clammy things which had once been their comrades into this hole they had made in the earth.

They were aware, too, of other things as they stood thus, as it were in suspended action; they knew, now, that what for these last long days had been filling their minds and absent from their speech… that hope at first faint then by sheer desire growing almost into a belief… they knew that now rescue was an improbability so wild as to be wellnigh impossible… This they knew and also a nearer and more immediate horror, foolishly far more to be dreaded than that other, that they could not, somehow, bury those bodies of their comrades as they were; that they must, however weak and sentimental and unnecessary this might be, not cover those bodies with the earth before that frightful transposition had been remedied and those staring, shocking faces made no longer obscene and bestial travesties but the features of Cook and MacKay.

The night, still and heavy and drenched around them with bars of black and silver, was silent with a silence which pressed upon them like a great weight. Each man of those three, Morelli lying with his eyes searching the desert, the Sergeant and Abelson standing on the lip of that grave, heard in his head this silence, broken only by the thud-thudding in their ears of their own hearts.

"God!" said the Sergeant, suddenly and beneath his breath. He tapped Abelson on the shoulder and swung round. "Come *on!*" he muttered, and crossed with rapid steps to where the still, white, dead things lay in their moon pool.

Abelson followed, more slowly. He saw the Sergeant stand a moment, looking down; saw his shoulders rise with a sudden taking of the breath; saw him kneel and put both hands to the face of the dead MacKay.

He came closer and slowly knelt by the side of that other body, facing the Sergeant, from whose lips came a stifled mutter, curses or prayer or self-exhortation… He looked down at what he himself must do; then suddenly stumbled to his feet and turned away. He said, aloud:

"No good… Can't do it… *Can't!*"

There was a silence behind him: it seemed to last for a year of dragging moments. Then the Sergeant's voice.

"That's that! Give us a hand!"

Abelson turned, reluctance clogging his movements. He did not mean to… he had determined that he *would* not… look down. But he did. His eyes of their own volition went straight to the bodies at the Sergeant's feet… And then he was flooded with inexpressible relief, for he saw that the moon now shone upon the faces of Cook and MacKay and did not lie, like a glistering lustre, upon faces which were not faces at all…

He stooped, and, stooping, dragged the great body of Cook across those intervening yards to the grave…

And soon there was no Cook, or MacKay… merely a slightly raised lump of newly-broken earth, beaten flat with boot and spade.

The Sergeant broke a long silence. "And how," he said, slowly and heavily, as a man will find himself speaking in a dream, "and how the hell did they *get* here?"

Abelson turned sharply. His mouth fell open; the little spade dropped from his hand. "By —!" he breathed. "Never thought… they were lyin' there just after that first shot…"

"Yes," the Sergeant said. "An' we were on the scene not more than a couple o' minutes later…"

159

"How do yeh…" Abelson's voice was awed and shaken and fragmentary; it uttered little bursts of words, each burst starting loud and tailing off to silence at its end. "But how the —! … Can't of *dropped* outa the… I tell yeh, Sergeant, it's—it's…"

"Unless, of course," came the Sergeant's voice. "*That's* it! That fool was asleep. That's it… Buddoo must 've dragged 'em up from over there… from somewhere… Sanders is asleep an' doesn't see 'em till they're close up … Must be that… If it isn't… then God help us all… But it *was* that."

A sigh broke from the Jew. "'S right!" he said. "Must be… The scab! … S'pose there'd been a dozen Buddoos, eh? What about *that*? … They'd of been all over us afore we knew it… The —!" His tone changed, suddenly. He turned, and his fingers clutched the Sergeant's wrist. He said, hoarsely: "What they bring 'em back here for? Eh? What *for*?"

The Sergeant shook his head wearily. "How the hell do *I* know… How would anybody know that… They're just bloody devils… that's all…" He laughed a little, a mirthless sound. "Bloody-minded devils!" he said. "They want… just to show us!" He turned slowly away from the grave. He seemed to shake himself and draw rigidly erect, with back-flung shoulders. He said, sharply, in a voice with an intensified parade-ground sharpness:

"Got to find Sanders! Get to it, Abelson. There'll be no guard to-night: we'll *all* be on."

"The soors won't come twice," Abelson said. "Not in one night."

"You find Sanders!" snapped the Sergeant. "You fool; never heard of a double bluff!" He walked off, back to where Morelli lay. Abelson, with a grimace, set off through the trees.

The Sergeant stood over Morelli. "Anything doin'?" he said.

"No... Fanny Adams... I got that sod, though." He pointed out across the gleaming sand to where that dark blotch still stained the silver.

"That's one of 'em," said the Sergeant. "But how many more are there? ... Two, I should say... P'r'aps three... No, maybe four or five because somehow they've been joined by the ones that caught Jock and Cook... An' as we didn't see any, God knows how many the total is now... But I don't think... it can't be more than five... if it was there'd 've been a pukka attack..." He broke off; was silent for a long moment; then added. "Stick here. Goin' to get my shirt. We'll all be with you peechi."

He walked quickly through the trees in the direction of the hut. As he saw it some ten or fifteen yards away, he heard the voice of Abelson.

"Sanders! Sand-ers! Where the hell *are* yeh? Speak up, you holy bahstud! Where *are* yeh?"

He saw, then, Abelson come out of the shadow to the eastward side of the hut and peer into it through one of those irregular holes which must be windows. He heard him cry, exultant: "*Kerm* out of it, you scab-faced —!"; saw him rush through the doorway and disappear.

And then, as he broke into a run, for he did not want Sanders knocked about, he heard a strange noise. A clattering. He checked his stride while his mind worked over this sound. He ran on again. It must be the swords. One of the two men had run into the little pile of eleven swords which had been in that corner since that night when first they had arrived here.

He smiled grimly at himself and the wild senseless imaginings which that metallic clattering had roused in him. He eased his run to a walk. Then, suddenly, he was racing, at the very top of his speed, across the few yards which still separated him from the hut. He had remembered that these swords had not been standing up so that they could be knocked down. They lay in a pile and therefore must have been deliberately raised before being dropped to make that noise.

So he ran. But not fast enough. When he was almost at that doorway, there came a sudden babel of sound from within: low, rasping, curses from Abelson, a high-pitched, crazy confusion of Biblical incoherence from the throat of Sanders. And then a hush, appalling in the rapidity with which it had fallen.

Out through the doorway, backwards, fell Abelson into the Sergeant's arms, which caught him.

"Steady up!" said the Sergeant's voice. "What the…"

He stopped; for the body in his arms was limp. He laid it down and a moonbeam showed a gaping hole where should have been the right eye and upper cheek…

And now through the doorway burst a figure, wild and babbling and three-quarters naked. It held in its hand, with a tense and dreadful awkwardness, an unsheathed cavalry sabre whose point was dark and sluggishly gleaming. The man's mouth drooled gouts and flecks of saliva between its shouted incoherent words.

It seemed to the Sergeant, looking up from the thing at his feet, that this other, live thing would attack him. He crouched and leapt. His hands caught the bony legs round each ankle. He straightened, keeping his hold. Sanders' head met the oven-baked ground with a thud which was almost a report. He too, lay still.

The Sergeant dropped upon his knees by the child-ishly huddled body of the Jew. He confirmed what he had known. Here, again, was death…

He stayed thus, upon his knees, for many black moments, staring with eyes which did not see into the black-shad-owed thickness of the trees. He felt numb; like a man who has been partially drugged with chloroform so that, while yet conscious, he is incapable alike of thought or action.

He was roused. From the trees came the sudden crack-crack of Morelli's rifle. Then four more shots and a voice, hailing.

He jumped to his feet and over the two still bodies, one dead and the other in unconsciousness as deep as death. He rushed into the hut and came out with two rifles, three laden bandoliers, and a water-bottle. He jumped over the bodies again and raced through the trees to where Morelli lay and cast himself down beside him.

Morelli was firing, steadily, irregularly; careful shots at definite targets. The Sergeant, too, began shooting. There was no need of words. Out on that glistening sand, away beyond the dark blotch which was the result of that earlier shooting of Morelli's, other black things were moving, coming from out that patch of protecting, unreasonable shadows… One… two… five… six black things, crawling.

They went on firing. Sparingly, with careful aim. But gradually, by almost infinitesimal stages, the six black things held to their advance.

"— it!" said Morelli savagely. "Can't we shoot a-tall. Or what? What you make the range?"

"Three-fifty, I've been at," the Sergeant said. "Think it's more." He slid up the sights.

"Um!" Morelli, nodding agreement, did the same. He fired again. One shot. "Where's that Yid?" he said.

The Sergeant fired. One shot. He said:

"He's not comin'. It's you an' me now."

"Eh?" Morelli's head jerked sharply round.

"You an' me, I said." The Sergeant pressed another clip into the magazine of his rifle. "Sanders is moost. Really moost. Stuck a sword through Abelson's eye… He's dead." He raised his rifle to his shoulder, cuddled his cheek down to the hard wood, and took careful aim at the first of those six black things which moved upon the shining glory of the desert.

XVIII

THREE... nearly four hours later. There is still a moon, but it is paling; the silver is turning to a light and ghostly grey... The Sergeant and Morelli are still lying there... But they are not firing... There are now, out there in front of them, only three dark blotches. And these are quiet and still: they are not crawling forward, even by stages infinitesimal. They will never, in fact, crawl anywhere again.

Round the left upper arm of Morelli there is tied, tightly, a wad of bandaging torn from the tail of his shirt. For he and the Sergeant have not had all the shooting to themselves. A ricochet caught him, the bullet glancing from a palm trunk and carving a groove from the flesh. Otherwise they are unhurt.

And, for the moment, victorious. The three... or was it four, as Morelli insisted... the living of their enemies had withdrawn into the impenetrable, unreasonable shadow.

Now that there was no longer need for attention utterly undivided, the Sergeant, as he lay, kept half-raising his naked neck and shoulders and peering behind him into the now lightening shadows of the trees.

"What *is* it?" Morelli said after the third time.

"Sanders."

Morelli started. "Christ! I'd forgotten... Not there, is he?"

"Can't see him," the Sergeant said. "That's why I was lookin'." He turned his head again.

Morelli, too, now twisted his body as he lay so that his eyes might peer into the drab shadows. He said:

165

"Buddoo in front; bloodthirsty bughouse wallah in the rear… Nice party we're havin', Sarge!"

They both laughed; short, strained, barking sounds.

The Sergeant said: "I *may* 've killed the poor sod… But I don't think so… Stood 'im on his head; had to…" He fell silent a moment while his gaze went out again over the desert before them. "There's Abelson, too," he added.

"More diggin'!" Morelli said. He began to giggle…

The Sergeant turned savagely. "Stop that blasted row! Stop it, will you!"

The choking laughter died away. "Sorry, Sarge!" Morelli said. "Dunno what's come over me. Oughta know better."

"Be dawn in a bit." The Sergeant's voice was again in its normal tones. "I want my shirt an' helmet. You stay here." He clambered stiffly to his feet, effacing himself from the desert behind a palm trunk. He turned and walked, rifle in hand, softly away.

"Watch your step, for Gawd's sake…" Morelli's voice floated after him. He walked on, smiling a twisted smile at this unnecessary advice. As he walked, his rifle was held slantwise beford him and the right forefinger was curled about the trigger. His body was carried tense and inclining forward from the hips. To his ears came sounds which were not sounds at all… creeping footsteps… harsh, insane breathing… the clink of a sword-blade against a tree… He caught himself saying, aloud: "Pull yourself *together*! You're not hearin' a damn thing!" He bit at his lips and walked on at a faster pace.

He came to the hut, and before it the body of Abelson. But there was no Sanders, nor any sight nor sound nor trace of Sanders. He stepped over that twisted body and, with an effort of will which left every muscle quivering, dashed into the darkness of the hut, rifle held protectingly above his head.

But there was no Sanders here…

He took from where they lay upon his blankets his shirt and topee and spine-pad. He thought: "Shall I put my shirt on here? Might come in an' get me when I'm all twisted up in it…"

He stood undecided a moment. Then the desire for that feeling of additional security which would come with the clothing made up his mind. He laid his rifle down upon the blankets and pulled the shirt over his head, snatching the weapon again so soon as this was done. He said, aloud:

"Jumpy as a cat!" and heard his voice as something rumbling and unnatural.

He tucked his shirt down into his breeches awkwardly with one hand; for the other held his rifle. His belt and its unbuckling and buckling was a difficult task with only five fingers. But it got itself done and he left the hut shirted and spine-padded and helmeted, and with two more laden bandoliers and a haversack swinging from his right shoulder.

As he came out of the doorway the dawn broke with a sudden rush of golden, glittering splendour. There was light everywhere and with it a solace for taut and jangled nerves.

But, at his feet, there lay Abelson's body… a reminder.

He stepped over it and walked towards the centre of the clearing, his eyes darting glances all about him. But of Sanders there was still no sign nor sound nor trace.

He came to a halt in the middle of the clearing, his eyes restless. There came to his ears Morelli's voice, shouting:

"Ser-geant! *Ser*-geant!"

"Right!" he cried back, and ran.

He came racing through the trees and cast himself down, sweating, in his old place. His eyes raked the desert; but found nothing save those three huddled bundles, seeming now, strangely enough, at a greater distance than they had in the soft silver blazing of the moonlight. "What's up?" he said. He did not turn his eyes to the man beside him.

Morelli said, stammering a little: "I… I… C'n you see anything… out… out there… Behind that third stiff?" He pointed. "Thought… could of sworn I… there was some'p'n moved…" Under his tan the dark blood covered face and neck with a fiery glow. He sent sidelong glances at the Sergeant's face and sighed almost audible relief to find that the eyes in that face were not upon his. For the truth was that Morelli had neither seen, nor even imagined himself to have seen, any such movement as he had described: it had merely come to him, after ten minutes alone which had seemed following that nightmare night to be an hour at the least, that something, probably Sanders, had happened to the Sergeant… He had fought this growing conviction for so long as he might, but had, at last, given way. That cry of "Sergeant! Sergeant!" had seemed to spring from his lips without intent. So soon as it had died away and there had come that answering shout he had felt, literally, that he would have given a hand to have kept silent…

Beside him, after long, dragging minutes, the Sergeant said:

"Can't see anythin'… Where're those glasses?"

There came, from behind them, the faint wraith of a sound. Both heard it, but neither spoke of having heard. They suspected themselves of nerves. But, though they did not speak, they stiffened, straining their ears. The Sergeant's question seemed still to hang suspended above them.

There… again that shadow of a sound… They both turned sharply… Morelli still lay gaping, his eyes wide, the blood ebbing from his face and leaving the tan a dirty, sickly grey. The Sergeant was on his feet almost in one movement. He stood, staring, breathing short and jerkily.

Before them, naked as a new-born child, stood Sanders… Naked and empty-handed… They who had pictured a murderer saw now a foolish saint.

He held out to them those empty hands, palms upwards. Upon his face was a smile which seemed of ineffable sweetness and then, after the first glance, froze a man with sick horror by its flaunting insanity.

The little group was motionless… utterly without a shadow of movement… for minutes which seemed a microcosm of eternity. They posed for some tableau devised by the great satirist.

Then Sanders moved. He came towards them with slow and delicate steps, those hands still supplicatory, the smile graven upon his features. He spoke; and the voice, deep and deliberately resonant, was so utterly unlike the voice which they knew that their first shock of incredulity and horror was surpassed by this second.

"I leave you," said the voice. "Ere I do so, kneel you and pray with me." He knelt, and clasped his hands, raising them high before his face. The eyes closed, but still the mouth was curved into that smile.

The voice again. "Our Father, which art in Heaven, hallowed be Thy name…"

The Sergeant came to life. His face was pale and carved with deep lines. He muttered: "Not decent… Stop it…" He came forward and put a hand, whose fingers shook, upon the naked, bony shoulder. He said, in a strange uncertain voice:

"That'll do now… That'll do!"

He was smitten, immediately after they had left his mouth, by the futile inadequacy of these words. He shook at the shoulder with iron fingers. "Get up now," he said. "Get up!"

He stooped suddenly and put a hand beneath each armpit of the kneeling figure and lifted it bodily to its feet. Certainty; his usual sureness; desire for a definite line of action; these had all, in a measure, returned to him.

Morelli, still staring wide-eyed from the ground, was thrown a curt: "You stay. Watch out there. Back peechi!" saw, before rolling over again upon his stomach, that nine-and-a-half-stone nakedness lifted like a child into the Sergeant's arms and carried off through the trees towards the hut. Even as he rolled over, so that once more his eyes should command the desert, he saw, with another horrified thrill, that over the Sergeant's retreating shoulder lolled and jerked that face with its smile which was not seraphic but so foolish as to seem an obscenity.

"God help us!" groaned Morelli, and lay once more looking out over that maddening infinite half-circle of once-more blazing, glaring sand.

It seemed to him a month of hours before there came footsteps behind him and the Sergeant's voice, pitched low to conceal the shrieking of his nerves.

"Anythin' doing?" it said.

Morelli, not looking up, shook his head. "No," he said. And his voice, even in his own ears was high and taut and unrecognisable.

The Sergeant lay down in his old place. They looked at each other for a fleeting second, then hastily away, as if each feared, as indeed he did, to find in the face of the other what he knew was written on his own.

The Sergeant wiped with wet hand at his streaming fore-head. He was breathing hard and quickly, almost panting: his hand shook and his lips moved one upon the other as if the thoughts which raced turgid through his head were striving after utterance too long denied.

Morelli pressed a dry tongue over drier lips. He asked: "What you do with 'im?" He had meant his voice to be calm and casual, but the little sentence came as a half-whispered croak.

"Hut," the Sergeant mumbled. "Tied 'im up... Three-four reins joined... round his middle, out through window, round a palm... Don't see how he *can* get away... Yet it oughtn't t' hurt 'im... Taken the swords an' all away; he can't cut the leather... an' I swear he'll not undo that raffle o' knots behind his back... He can move about, too... An' I've left him dates an' water... He's still prayin'; *with* that smile..." His voice died away.

Morelli was silent.

The Sergeant burst out at him. "Well! Had to do it, didn't I? He won't put any clothes on... Can't let 'im wander round spare an' the sun just gettin' up... What else *could* I do? Eh? Tell me! What else?"

Morelli said, quickly, so that his words tripped and stumbled one upon the heels of the other:

"Sure! Sure! Had to tie 'im up. Sure! But I was just thinking..." He cut his speech off abruptly.

"Thinkin' what?"

"Thinking that... that... Well, now... I... I was just wond'ring... wouldn't it be best all round if... if... well, sod it! if we was to put the pore guy out of his trouble? Wouldn't it, now?"

"Thought o' that," said the Sergeant. Then, turning, he shot out: "Who's goin' to do it? Would you?"

Morelli flinched. He was a man of some imagination. He did not speak again, but lay staring straight out before him.

"Would you?" came the Sergeant's voice, insistent.

Morelli shook his head, slowly. "No," he muttered. "Not now as I come to think of it... Not but what it wouldn't be right as we're all goin' to be for the high jump... But *I* couldn't. No, sir!"

"Nor me..." the Sergeant said. "I *thought* of it... An' then I looked at the poor devil... Sittin' there, smilin' like that, and prayin' away... Damn it, Morelli, I believe I *would* 've done it if he'd been *dressed*!"

"Ah!" Morelli nodded. "... What about some grub?"

The Sergeant passed, from where it lay beside him in the haversack, the half of the wad of picked and squeezed-together dates which he had carried with him on his last return from the hut.

They ate, chewing in silence and washing down the fruit with tepid water from the bottles. They finished the meal and the Sergeant examined his cigarette-case. "Five," he said. "How many you?"

"Three," Morelli said, "but... there's Abelson's..." He passed one to the Sergeant and put another to his own mouth.

Smoke curled lazy above their heads: it hung like infant clouds in the shimmering air. With almost every minute the heat grew more savage, and always with a threat of worse to come.

Morelli broke a long silence. "Sergeant..." he said, "ever hear tell of Jonahs?"

"Yes." The Sergeant nodded. His attention seemed to wander. "Wish to God," he muttered, "those devils 'd *do* something... This waiting!"

Silence.

"About Jonahs..." came Morelli's voice. "You listening?"

"Yes," said the Sergeant. "Yes."

"I'm one!" Morelli's voice was low-pitched and slow. "Here... I'll tell you..."

XIX

THEY dug, by turns, away on the far side of the hut, a grave for Abelson. The Sergeant put the body in and piled the earth atop of it and stamped it down.

A day passed; a night... another day and another night.

Time ceased for these two men. Its harsh man-made divisions melted in the sun's furnace and the silver bath of the moon. They ate now and then; they drank much water. They slept in turn, fitfully or not at all. By turn they beat down dates to renew their store and drew water. By turn they walked dazedly to the hut and gave food and drink to the naked madman who prayed there, smiling; who suffered himself to be led out, like a beast, for exercise; whose only words to his keepers were: "I leave you... kneel you and pray with me!"

At times they talked, sometimes in monosyllables, sometimes loquaciously for hours together. Once they were silent for so long as it takes the sun to make his circuit. But always they watched, with eyes that burned and ached and wept from the glare of the sun or the glinting of the moon. It seemed to them that for their whole lives... for the whole of time... they had been lying thus upon their bellies, with elbows worn and torn by propping their weight, looking out over Nothing with aching, burning eyes; waiting for an enemy they dared not seek and could not see but whose existence was a fact; a magic enemy who hid where was no hiding-place, who brought back, hideously defaced, the bodies of their friends to lie and foully mock them; who would eventually conquer them as those others had been conquered.

Their eyes were coals. Over their dark faces grew stubbled beards. Though their lair was in a measure shaded, the heat thrashed at them like a savage animal, so that each sun cycle was a crescendo of fire with a night in its wake scarcely more tolerable. The wooden stocks of their rifles burnt their hands, and the metal parts were agony to touch. Always, ceaselessly, their bodies poured out sweat until it seemed to them that soon they must utterly dissolve. They felt, at times, that their sanity was leaving them. Around and above them, tall, minatory sentinels, were the palms, unstirred, unmoving always. Before them was that aching semi-circle of nothingness; a barren furnace by day, a leprous silver bowl by night. The nothingness grew in their minds to a fevered, lustful, inimical personality which hated them and would send them madness before death.

"If only something 'd *move*!" Morelli groaned. "*Any* bloody thing!"

The Sergeant turned on an elbow. He had been silent for nearly a day; now the speech came frothing out of him like an angry torrent. He said, nearly shouting:

"Yes. Yes. I know. Somethin' ought to move. Yes. But what ought to move? Eh? Why, those bloody devils! — em, I say! Cod rot 'em and blister their blasted souls! They'll get us! But by the bones o' their Prophet, we'll get them, too! Ever had Ambition, Morelli? 'Course you have! So've I. Not one, but a thousand of 'em. I've had it bad in my time, Morelli. But by God I've never had it as I've got it now. I'll get those swine! I'll get 'em, I tell you! I'll get 'em. An' then I'll die…" His voice ceased; he had suddenly become aware that he was shouting loud and louder, at a man so near that a whisper would have reached him. And his own voice, its strange tone, still rang unpleasantly in his ears. He bit at his lip and strove for composure.

But now Morelli, infected, was shouting back:

"… all very well. All very ruddy well. But why're them soors waitin'? Why? I'll tell you. Just come to me, an' if we wasn't goin' bughouse lying here we'd 'a' seen it long ago. They're waitin' for some pals. Get me? Bleeding reinforcements. That's what! We pipped three the other night, didn't we! That leaves three more: p'r'aps four. They're not going to chance it. Why? 'Cos they *knows* their little brown brothers 're comin'. Then they'll mop us up. Easy too. Jam from the bloody baby, it'll be. Your ambition's goin' t' hell. Ain't it now? Eh?"

"All right. All right. You needn't shout!" The Sergeant had regained composure; his voice was low again, and even and incisive. "You may be right. You're logical anyhow. But *I* think you're wrong, in spite o' the probabilities. I tell you: I think they're waiting… just because they're waiting. Part of their programme. Follow me? They're not just straight out to kill us. They're *enjoyin'* 'emselves. Look at the way they brought Jock back, an' the Matlow. See what I'm gettin' at? This waitin's just another bit o' fun an' games."

"Dunno… maybe you're right…" Morelli, too, had sobered now. "Hell's bells! What's it matter which way it is? — 'em all! An' us too!" He began to whistle, dolorously:

"They're hangin' men and women now for wearin' o' the Green."

The Sergeant took it up. The plaintive tune floated up into the palms; died away.

"Nothin' like music," said the Sergeant. He grinned suddenly and began to sing:

> "Oh! Landlord have you some good red wine?
> *Parley-voo!*
> Oh! Landlord have you some good red wine?
> *Parley-voo!*
> Oh! Landlord have you some good red wine
> Fit for the Cavalry of the Line?
> What-ho, ye bleeders!
> What-ho, ye bleeders!
> *What-ho!"*

Morelli stared at him, listening, at first vacuously, then with interest, finally with a great grin which split in two his stubble-covered face. He yelled suddenly, with a shrieking yodel which might well have been heard, in that silence, two miles away:

"Let 'er rip, then. Atta-bohoyee!"

He burst into the second verse, his rather strident tenor mingling, not without harmony, with the Sergeant's deep baritone.

> "Oh! Landlord, have you a daughter fine?
> *Parley-voo!*

Oh! Landlord, have you a daughter fine?
Parley-voo!
Oh! Landlord, have you a daughter fine
Fit for the Cavalry of the Line?
What-ho, ye bleeders!
What-ho, ye bleeders!
What-ho!"

The palms rang with the swinging, martial tune. The words and cadences soared up and out across the desert, now red with the crimson blood of the dying sun. They looked at each other, smiling, and sang the harder. They got from their bellies to their knees, from their knees to their feet. They faced each other, heads flung back, roaring out verse after verse, each verse louder than its predecessor. The blood mounted to their heads and darkened their dark and bearded faces. The sweat ran from their foreheads, their cheeks; down their chests and backs.

The song came to its end. The Sergeant panted: "Stuff to give 'em. Nothin' like music…"

And Morelli: "Yeah… give 'em… "Fred Karno's Army"… Right:

"We are Fred Karno's A-armee,
No bleedin' good are we-ee!
We cannot fight; we cannot shoot;
What God-damn' use are we-ee?
An' w'en we get to Ber-lin,
Ther Kayser, he will sa-ay,

179

'Och! Och! Mein Gott!
What a — — lot
Are the n-teenth Cavalree!"

That gave them more breathing space, for this song is sung to the tune of a famous hymn, and is slow and solemn and swelling. They began, being thus still in breath, upon a song which Hale had been used to sing. It was called "True Love" and its first line ran:

"I-ee want Justice! was all ther Young Sylor said!"

They broke down half-way through that, in an argument concerning words and tune. They still stood. They grew heated and began to shout.

"Chubbarow!" roared the Sergeant. "What's it matter? Give 'em 'Leapfrog'!"

Once more they flung back their heads and roared out tune and words. This time the noise surpassed even that of "Fred Karno's Army." The very trees seemed to shake to their voices. And, as if abashed by this vigour, the sun's gory blaze paled gradually.

"*They* were only playin' LEAP-frog,
They were only playin' LEAP-frog,
They were only playin' LEAP-frog,
As one grasshopper jumped right over the other grasshopper's back!"

They sang till their necks swelled and the veins upon them stood out like cords. They sang up into the trees and then out, hands trumpeting their mouths, across the desert, blood-red no longer but tinted now as if by fading light stealing through a stained glass window. They turned and sang it at each other. Morelli danced now, fantastic heel and toe, as he sang; the Sergeant beat with his arms in furious travesty of conducting…

They sang themselves out. They dropped and lay, panting and sweating. Morelli began, between gasps, to laugh. This laughter grew. It bubbled and choked and bubbled again. It infected the Sergeant so that presently he too was laughing. They rolled from stomach to back, from back to side, laughing…

The Sergeant sat up and rubbed with his knuckles at his streaming eyes. He stayed a while staring out at the desert, where nothing moved nor was save sand and those three huddled bundles. Gettin' highish by now, he thought… and began to laugh again.

Morelli said, suddenly sobered: "His nibs… whose turn?" He jerked a thumb vaguely in the hut's direction.

"Mine," the Sergeant said, and stopped laughing. "Yes … I'll get along… in a minute."

"Thank God it's not me!" Morelli's voice was barely louder than a whisper now. "It's all this looking after *him* that gets *me*!"

"Ah; it's none too pleasant." The Sergeant too had lowered his tone. "Better 'n if it'd been one o' the others, though…"

Morelli looked at him. "You're right there!" he said slowly. "Never thought of that… That's right… Suppose it'd been ole Topper! … He was a good guy, that!"

The Sergeant nodded. "He was… So were the others … all of 'em in their own ways… Man couldn't wish for a better lot… 'cept *him*…"

"You're right, Sarge… an' I can't help this Jonah business…"

"Bloody fool!" the Sergeant growled.

"Yes." Morelli's voice went on, "'s good a bunch o' guys as you'd find. Better. Even ole Abey had guts. Yessir; a double ration o' guts, Abey had… Yes; been a helluva sight more gaga 'f any o' *them* 'd gone moost… *He* always was half anyways…" He broke off, to say, seconds later: "*Good Gorralmighty!*"

"What's that?" The Sergeant turned quickly.

Morelli, his face only half-visible by reason of the shadow and the dusk that was now beginning to enwrap the world, seemed to gape, open-eyed, wide-mouthed. He said:

"It's just… thinkin' about Topper natcherly made me think of climbing them trees… An' I've remembered! There wasn't no need for all that chucking lines an' all that… You just loop a rope round the tree and tie it under y'r seat and hitch yourself up… Easy…"

"But what about it?" the Sergeant said. "I remembered that… after. But it wouldn't 've made any difference."

"No. Reckon not… Why it struck me like… I was thinking maybe 'f we'd thoughta that we could a had a look-out, permanent…"

"Chuck that, for Mike's sake!" The Sergeant's voice cut savagely through the dusk. "What's the good o' chewin' the rag about what we *could* have done? No use at all! If we'd had a look-out, what'd 'ave happened? We'd all 've been pipped a damn' sight quicker; that's all…"

Morelli said hurriedly: "Right y'are, Sarge. Right…"

But the Sergeant's voice went on. "P'r'aps we've… *me*, if you like! … p'r'aps *I've* done everything right; or everything wrong; or some right an' some wrong… But I've done what I've done. And that's bloody well all there bloody well is to it! Get me? P'r'aps we'd 've done better not to let Jock and Cook go! P'r'aps we'd 've done better not to 've used the roof as a day look-out! P'r'aps we ought never, though there are only two of us, have stopped usin' it! P'r'aps we ought to 've tried, right at the start, to rush that invisible nullah those Arabs 're in! P'r'aps we ought to 've chanced attractin' more Buddoos an' had a flag up, or a bloody great smoke-fire goin' all the time 'case any o' the rest of the British bloody Army 'd seen us! P'r'aps this! P'r'aps that! An' p'r'aps the — other! But what I've done I've done, an' what I haven't I haven't! And that, my lad, is *that*! An' f'r the love of the Holy Ghost let it *be* that!"

He cut off this speech as suddenly as he had begun it. He lay, peering out before him, eyes battling with the dimness, breath coming hard and fast.

Silence held them. The dusk gave way to darkness; the darkness almost immediately to the first gleaming rays of the dying moon.

The Sergeant said, his voice low:

"Sorry, Morelli! Shouldn't 've let fly like that…"

"*That's* all right, Sarge!" Morelli said. "Forget it. My fault."

"No. Mine. But it's… I went off the deep end like that because… well, because I've had to do the thinkin' in this business, an' I've had to meet all these things as they came came along. An' it seems somehow as if everything I had to do had five or six alternatives. An' I've twisted my head silly, thinkin'…"

"Good job for us you were with us," said Morelli quickly.

The Sergeant grinned with a sudden flash of white teeth against the wellnigh invisible darkness of his face. "Thanks. Cut it out… Look here! Tell you what gets me most … It's bein' done in by a lousy set of Arabs. That's what! What's this war to them? Why, they might just as easily 've been friendly. Some are; some aren't. An' they don't make up their black bloody minds till they see how many men they've got to deal with. — 'em!"

"Me too," Morelli said. "Wouldn't get me so mad 'f they was Turks… But Buddo! I joined up to get a whack in at Jerry. 'Cos why? One: because I'm English in spite o'my Wop monaker. Two: because I always have hated the lousy Germans. An' hero I am, about to be dessicayted by a lot o' stinkin' poxy Arabs… I'm a Jonah to meself, too, that's one comfort." He stopped; then burst out on a note which was a sort of whispered wail:

"An' what's going to come to Moree?"

It was as if the words had been torn from his mouth by some ruthless, invisible hand. Almost whispered though they were, they seemed to tear their way through the darkness and strike the Sergeant's ears like flame-tipped arrows.

"That your partner?" He said the words for the sake of speech.

"Ah; Joey," came the whisper. "Thank God we'd put enough money by… But she'll want *me*! Me! … Lyin' there… on her back for always, always…" His voice changed; grew loud and over-gruff. "Aw, hell!" he said. "What's the good… But I guess you'll maybe know how I'm feeling, Sarge."

"I do!" the Sergeant said.

Morelli turned his head. "Got someone who'll be needing you?"

"No." The tone was curt. "Not a soul. There's one who'll p'r'aps think so… for a bit… But she… they'll be better off." He got quickly to his feet. "Yes. Better off by a damn long chalk." He stooped and picked his rifle from where it had lain beside him. "Go an' see to *him* now," he said. "Give us the bottles. I'll fill 'em."

He walked slowly away, rifle under one arm; water-bottles slung from the other shoulder. Morelli watched until the tall trees and their latticed shadows had swallowed him.

XX

HALF-WAY to the hut, the Sergeant changed his mind and his direction. He would, after all, go first to the spring and fill the two bottles which he carried. Sanders could wait for that further three minutes.

He strode across the clearing, a wry smile twisting his mouth: he sneered at himself for childish postponement of unpleasing duties.

He came to the spring and laved his face and neck and cupped water in his palms and drank. He took the first bottle and began to fill it.

The moon-washed silence which clothed the world like a mantle was rent, with that appalling yet inevitable suddenness with which all silence must be broken, by the jarring rattle of four shots from Morelli's rifle.

The bottle fell from the Sergeant's hands. He snatched up his own rifle and raced back to the clearing and across it. He heard, faintly, other shots, the ghosts of their reports. He ran on, his ears aching expectant.

But no sound came to them.

He burst through the trees, his lungs labouring, his heart thudding in his ears. He came to the place… he could have found it blindfold by this… where Morelli should have been.

But no Morelli was there.

He threw himself down in what had become his form. His gaze went out, seeking, over that silver waste. His lungs fought for ease. The sweat ran down from his forehead; salt and stinging it blurred his vision. He rubbed savagely at his eyes so that at last they saw.

Away out before him, a hundred yards or more, was Morelli. He was running in short, erratic curves. He pursued another figure... a figure whose nakedness shone in the dusk light like a leper's skin.

The Sergeant came to his feet in a single movement. He shouted, with all the force of his lungs.

"Morelli! Come back, Morelli! ... Leave him! ... Back, you bloody fool! *Back!*"

If Morelli had heard him, he gave no sign. By a cunning swerve he came at last up to Sanders and clutched at him and held him.

"Back!" roared the Sergeant. "*Come back! Leave him!*"

But still, out there in the moonlight, the figures wrestled.

Now those faint reports began once more, and little spurts of sand shot up round and about the figures.

The Sergeant, helpless, watched; saw the naked, shining figure suddenly relax and sink, shutting up like a jack-knife, to the ground; saw Morelli, after one glance, turn and come racing back.

"Come *on!*" the Sergeant shouted. He began himself to fire, rapidly, towards that shadow from which the bullets that played about the little running figure seemed to come.

Morelli came near and nearer. The Sergeant, holding his breath, went on firing.

Near... nearer... So near that now the Sergeant could see his face, the mouth open, contorted with effort; the eyes wide and staring.

"Come on! You've done it. *Come on!*" he yelled at the runner.

But, half-way up the slope, Morelli stopped; turned slowly and languidly about, and fell upon his face. The action, by its slow mockery of grace, was appalling.

The Sergeant flung down his rifle, crawled upon his belly down the slope, seized those heels so foolishly cocked and dragged, inch by inch, the body back into the trees. Three bullets cut up the earth beside him on this journey; and then, back in the shadow, he was safe.

He knew, even before he stooped to examine, that Morelli was dead... And out there, shining, was the crumpled, naked body of the madman, who, by his escape, had left one man alone.

XXI

THE night passed. The shafts of the sun, coming laterally through the trees, flooded the clearing with a hard, bright light.

The clearing was empty of life. Or would have seemed so. A man standing in its centre and casting his glance around him would have had his eye arrested by the mutti hut, nestling among the earlier ranks of trees upon the south-western side; would have noticed immediately, by the glinting of the sun upon them, the two rifle barrels which protruded from the little irregular window-hole; would have seen, with the inner eye, the two men who knelt within the hut, invisible, and held their rifles to their shoulders.

But there was no man in that little house. The Sergeant, indeed, was within the clearing. Just within it. He lay in a shallow pit on that side by the spring, facing the hut's eastern end. He had worked hard to make this pit. It lay at the foot of a palm and was cunningly disguised, being sometimes more, sometimes less covered by shadows and having disposed before it most ingeniously palm fronds which lay as if fallen.

He lay upon his belly within this pit. Under his right hand was his rifle. Under his left two strands of unravelled rope. Three strands ran out of the pit, along the ground behind tree trunks and so into the hut through its doorway. There they joined other lines in such manner that, providing his hasty mechanics were sound, the jerking of one would cause the two rifles within his sight to fire and that of the other those two rifles which were thrust from the other window.

With him in the pit, beside these things, were an entrenching tool; a little stack of ammunition, the clips neatly piled; three water-bottles, full; a haversack holding a pile of dates; a jack-knife, open; and a sword without its scabbard.

All through the night, since Morelli's death, he had laboured. First at the pit, then at the arrangement of those four rifles in the hut. This latter work he had thought would never be needed. There was the pack-saddle rope to be unravelled, the rifles arranged with props made from saddlery and swords, the lines to be calculated and tied and tested and hidden on their journey to his lair… this he had taken hours which seemed to him twice three times their length.

But all his preparations now were done. There was nothing before him but waiting. He lay there and became, it seemed to him, an Ear. The sun mounted in the brazen sky; it topped the palm trees at his back and beat down upon the world and him.

He waited.

Time ceased for him. Though his eyes had not closed throughout the night there came to him neither sleep nor the desire for sleep. It cannot be said that while he waited he thought, for to think is a conscious exercising of the brain. He did not consecutively think, then; but all the time his mind was filled with pictures and a something else which served for these pictures as a background… a sheet upon which this cinematograph performance which was going on inside his head... a performance continuous but having no relevance between one picture and the next... a sheet which served the double purpose of holding the pictures and giving to them all a brooding, ultimate purpose; weaving, as it were, their seeming irrelevances into a pattern of meaning.

This screen was his Ambition. The word flashed into his mind, upon the screen which was itself, and he seized upon it. It was, he found, not the right word. Yesterday it might have been, and on those days between yesterday and the theft of the horses, it certainly would. But not now. Ambition was too small, too puny, too indecisive a definition. Ambition meant a wish, a desire to attain some particular object; it did not cover such feelings, such... such *possessions* as that which now had hold of him. He remembered... how long ago was it? ... he remembered saying something to Morelli about it: he'd said that there was an ambition in him, growing, an ambition like no other he had ever had, to get these swine of Arabs before he finally kicked the bucket... That was the first time he'd opened his mouth about this thing which had been burning inside him ever since that first day... The first and only time...

But it had been in him all the while, growing with a fierce and rapid and alarming growth. He could trace it, when he frowned and clenched his teeth and by effort of will stopped the pictures from coming and made real thought take their place... He could trace it: first a wish, half-ironic;

then definite desire; then ambition; then a small flame, hot within him, of longing; now a consuming, raging, stifling Determination… He would. He would! He *would* do this thing to which he had set himself!

His body stiffened as he lay. He half-raised himself on an elbow. His fingers tightened themselves like rope wires about the barrel of the rifle beside him. He said aloud:

"I will. I will. I *will*!"

The sound of his own voice struck strangely upon his ears, so long strained to catch other sounds than this. He had not known that he was speaking. The voice was so odd that he tried it again. He bowed in the direction of the hut.

"Good-morning!" he said. And this sound was stranger than before. He shook his head savagely, like an animal in pain. He tried once more.

"It's a damn funny thing how funny a man's own voice sounds when he starts talkin' to himself!"

He listened to this while he said it, carefully. It seemed more rational. He found that to hear himself speak was rather pleasant than otherwise. He began to chat. He said:

"Can't be much longer now… An' then the balloon goes up. Must've been just before dawn thought I saw those three ride out from that shadow. That means they're goin' to circle an' come in from different ways… they know I can't cover all points… but they don't know I'm not even tryin' to, blast 'em! Show the — pigs they're not the only fly ones! Yes. That's it. Yes! … My God, it's bloody hot… man does nothing but sweat… I'm soakin'… Come *on*, you *sods*!

"… Wonder they never tried that ridin 'an' circlin' business before. Must've had their horses there! Didn't want to lose *them*, I s'pose… But they've been a long time now… Part o' the programme? Yes. That's it. Yes! … One thing, though… wish to God I knew exactly how many visitors I'm goin' to get… They'll all come on *this* call… Soors! Now there's only one left… they'll *all* come, but is it three or four? Now more'n four, if that. Yes… *I* think there were three there an' then four caught Jock an' the Matlow an' brought 'em back an' then killed 'em… Then we pipped three… or was it four… say three… leaves four… Yes. That's it. Four. Yes. Yes! I'll be ready for 'em, *I* will. Yes."

The voice was growing louder and louder, the words pouring out in a bubbling torrent.

"Bloody swine! Festering lot of poxed-up niggers! I *will* get 'em. I will, I will! Yes, by God! … Wonder which way they'll come… If any come from the back here, the tree'll hide me a bit. Yes… Ought to see two of 'em over that side 'fore they see me in my little hole. My little hole! My little hole! A bright little tight little trenchlet! Oh! what a nice little cess-pit! A dear little…"

Suddenly he heard himself. Became aware, too, that now he was kneeling; that his voice was a hoarse, raving shout; that, mad, he had thrown aside his topee and that the sun was beating full down upon his unprotected head.

"My Christ!" he whispered. "My *Christ*!" He snatched up one of the water-bottles, jerked out its cork and tipped its contents over his head and neck. He reached out and snatched his helmet and rammed it back upon his head.

He lay hidden again, trembling. He took a firm grip upon himself. He relaxed his tautened, quivering muscles and breathed slow and deep.

He vowed to himself that his lips should not speak again… until his visitors arrived.

He passed a damp hand along his cheek and jaw. The touch seemed to please him, for he smiled… He had, before dawn, at the end of those labours of the night, done a curious thing. He had washed himself and shaved; shaved as clean as if he were to be, an hour later, upon a ceremonial parade. And after shaving he had turned to his uniform. It was stained and greasy and torn; but with it he had done his best. Spurs, shining, were upon his boots. His puttees were neat and tight. His shirt was settled well about him, close and trim across breast and shoulders, tucked tightly down into his breeches; then the leather belt about his waist had been newly soaped; its buckles polished with sand and water. Across his shoulders, empty for the sake of comfort, was his bandolier, its leather clean, its little brass pouch-studs glistening… Beneath him, in his little pit, was even a folded blanket, so that sand should not mar his attempt at parade-ground order…

It had taken him, this poshing, nearly an hour. He had done it swiftly, silently; automatically almost. Ever and again, as he scoured or scraped or rubbed, his lips, free now from their long growth of itching stubble, had made the muttered words:

"Filthy lot o' swine… Dung-heap savages! …"

He lay still now... still as death... There could not ... *could* not... be much more of this waiting. He strove for calm and attained it. A curious calm: his body was relaxed and easy, though under the battering of the sun the sweat ran from him in streams now warm, now clammily cold. A curious inexplicable calm; for his ears were straining, straining, and his mind had taken once more to that business of picture-making...

Perhaps this strange peace was not despite but due to these pictures in his head; for though behind these there was still that screen of his obsession, his determination, the pictures themselves were not, as they had been before, of Morelli and Sanders; Cook and MacKay naked and vilely misused; the empty horse-line with little Pearson huddled before it; Bell dead across the threshold of the hut; scenes in which, by following other courses to those he had taken, he had brought those men of his safely and triumphantly out of this mess... No. Now the pictures were of matters belonging to that other life, that life before this war for which one had enlisted, fervently, to destroy Germans, only to be put to lingering deaths by syphilitic savages. They started, it is true, with a picture of his mare so recently stolen by these same savages... lovely, eager; coat shining in the sun glare; soft, tender nostrils blown comically, sweetly, out to greet him; one slender foreleg picking daintily at the baked sand... but quickly this picture had changed to that of another, more beloved mare: Kitty, her name was, and she had borne him over many, many miles of that many-miled continent of South America... If only Kitty now were here...

But Kitty had faded. Inconsequently had come pictures of that day, over twenty years ago, when the Great Row had come at home... His father had been wrong ... he still held to this... utterly wrong to kick out into the world, without a penny, a boy of sixteen... just because of *that*... But still, now for the first time, he thought he would like, perhaps, to see the old boy... after all, that kicking-out had led to things: times hard and hellish hard; but goodish times too, some very good... and things had been done...

But the Governor faded. A jumble came then. His first job, a second footman... not bad this for a lad just out of the Upper Fifth... His second job... that was a bad one. His third, second under-assistant-deputy steward on a fourth-rate B.A. boat. Then South America... Then... flicker-flick... the tea job in Assam... flicker... the girl Dolores in Rio, that shawl wrapped tight about her slim, swaying body. Flick! ... that crash over the Sports Ground mortgage. A fortune missed there, by just the half of a split hair... flicker... the operator's turning the damned handle too fast... Shooting the man Faire and beating it up-country *quick*... the amazingly funny business about Hardman and Sons in Denver... Restless, restless! ... Some going almost too quick to know 'em except vaguely.

Then... oh! God! ... Noël! Noël in that dark green dress, waving to him from the quay; he could see the soft sparkle of the tears that stood in her eyes and were not allowed to fall; see the sun, kindly and benevolent glinting on the red-gold hair beneath the fine sweep of the hat brim. And beside her was Michael. He, too, was waving... a grin on his face but curses of joy in his heart...

Noël... Noël... what wouldn't he give to see...

The pictures ceased. His ears had caught a sound. The ghost of a sound. There was nothing definite to which he could ascribe that sound. But sound it was: a difference, just, from the aching silence which had seemed a part of him and the world.

The Sergeant's heart leaped within him. Fingers shaking with excitement, he pressed up the safety-catch on his rifle. He burrowed deep and deeper into his pit. His ears strained now for sound as surely no ears had ever strained before. His eyes, just now dull and glazed and inward-gazing, jumped into life; they shone and glittered. His mouth smiled a twisted smile. There had suddenly flashed into his head a memory of Morelli, starting up in his sleep, shouting "Ten Little Nigger Boys."...

There! The sound again... And again... The Sergeant waited, hardly breathing. Morelli came into his mind once more; he had a sudden urgent wish that they should not find Morelli's body where he had hidden it... He hoped to God they wouldn't! Hoped to God! ...

He started. More sounds had come... He could have sworn... Yes... it was a voice. A thick, muttering voice...

He was suddenly icy calm. The excited trembling left him.

He raised, half-inch by half-inch, smoothly his head. He peered through his little screen of palm fronds. He saw; and a great wave of elation surged through him. He felt Power. He felt as God. He had willed them to lay themselves in his hands. They had obeyed.

He saw them plainly; three of them. Two were standing, tall, gaunt, vilely sombre in their dun-coloured robes, directly opposite to where he lay. They were back to back, darting glances this way and that. In their hands were long, queerly-shaped rifles. He saw that from where they stood the hut was invisible. The third lay flat, some ten yards to that side of the two farther from the hut.

Of the standing two he could see the faces. Swarthy, handsome, bestial; one was deeply pock-marked.

The Sergeant's left hand crept towards the two strings, closed over one, over both, suddenly jerked…

His mechanics had been sound. There was rattling, deafening, rippling roar, as the four rifles fired from the hut, the bullets of the two from the side facing the clearing rattling high among the feathered palms.

As one, the standing Arabs leapt round to face the sound of the shots: the lying one, too, turned his body.

The Sergeant, exultation flooding him, came to his feet, for as he lay he could not fire with certainty. The rifle at his shoulder spat. The taller of the standing Arabs crumpled, twisted; fell and did not move. The Sergeant… it was all as quick as light… fired again. The second Arab tottered, dropped his long rifle and came to his knees…

The rifle at his shoulder spat.

The Sergeant, turning, fired again, now at the Arab who lay and even now was firing at him. As his finger pressed the trigger he felt something like a great blow, struck with a padded hammer, take him in the left thigh…

He fell, gripping his rifle… Groaning, he raised himself to a knee to see that he had won the duel; his shot must have got home between the eyes; there was no man lying there now, but a huddled lifeless heap.

But there was yet the second Arab, who, kneeling, strained, enfeebled by the anguish of his wound, to reach his fallen rifle… strained and succeeded.

The Sergeant, pain sweeping in great waves over him, slowly turned… He looked, across the clearing, straight into a rifle muzzle which wavered, then was steady… Again two shots sounded as one… Again a blow from a padded Miölnir flung the Sergeant down… This time it was his left shoulder and breast… He fumbled with a wavering, unsteady hand, to find a gaping breach of a wound. His lips, close to the dust, whispered:

"Dum-dum!"

He knew before consciousness left him, that again the winning shot had been his; the Arab who had knelt was now another shapeless heap…

The Sergeant lay huddled at the lip of his little pit. His eyes were closed, his mouth open with down-dropped lower jaw. His left thigh was broken, and his left shoulder, beneath which, spreading down to the ribs, was that gaping, dreadful wound. His rifle lay beside him…

He knew nothing… and blood poured from him. He was utterly still… still as the three who shared the clearing with him…

From among the trees behind him came a sound. Such a ghost of a sound as, five minutes before, he had heard with such delight. But now he could not hear…

The sound came again, stealthily. A figure rose from the ground among the trees. A tall figure clad in dun-coloured robes; out from its kaftan looked a fierce brown face, handsome and bestial. It carried a long, oddly-shaped rifle…

A tremor ran through the body of the Sergeant. At the closed doors of his consciousness there was a knocking… a knocking… it thundered in his head…

Wearily, with agony and reluctance, those doors swung open. In his head, all through him now, a word went pulsing:

"Three! Three! Three!"

He fought for the strength to open his eyes. Slowly the lids rose. He screamed, but with no voice, as the sun struck flaming spears into his head. But his eyes stayed open.

"Three! Three! Three!" thundered through his head, his body, his tortured wounds.

And then understanding came back. He knew, now, what this "Three" had meant.

"Oughta been four… least!" His dust-caked mouth formed the words without sound… Without volition, his right arm moved, its hand seeking a pocket… The fingers closed over that little automatic. Its butt felt cold and heavy…

"Three…" said his lips. "P'r'aps… only… aft'rall…"

And then… a shadow. A shadow which came between him and the sun…

"Four. Four. Four-four-four!" hammered his pulses.

He waited… He bit with feeble teeth at his befouled lower lip. Bit hard for strength; bit hard to keep back the groan that the agony of his wounds, now that life was with him again, was forcing up from his lungs…

He waited, eyes spying from under lids three-quarters closed… He held his breath.

The shadow lengthened; grew less…

Over him stood a figure, a hand fumbling for knife among the folds of its burnous…

The Sergeant made strength… or borrowed from source unknown. He rolled suddenly over, on to his left side, upon his wounds… In a sweep, his right hand came from his breeches' pocket… The automatic spoke its stuttered speech… to the full.

The Arab swayed, collapsed… fell with lurching crash; dead before his shoulders hit the ground.

The Sergeant's voice came back to him.

"Four!" he cried in a high, thin voice. "Knew it!"

He climbed, with a frightful effort of will, to one knee. His face was contorted, unrecognizable… He got, some-how, to his feet…

He stood, swaying, borne up by some power within or without himself, upon his leg that was not injured. He looked down upon this fourth.

"Dog!" he said, "swine!" A cough shook him, tore at him. A rattling cough… Blood welled faster from that yawning hole where his left breast should have been.

He swayed, wildly, almost falling.

"T-t-ten… l-little… nig' boys!" he said.

"An'… then… then there… were none!"

He fell, face downwards, across the body of the Arab.

GLOSSARY

Asti: steady! Go easy (from Hindustani)

Bandolier: a belt worn across the shoulder with loops or pockets for cartridges

Bibi: woman; girl (from Hindustani)

Boos: sole, only (from Hindustani)

Buckle: Jew (rhyming slang, *buckle-my-shoe*)

Buddoo: Arab

Budgi: time; *lit.* hour (from Hindustani)

Burnous: a long, loose hooded cloak worn by Arabs

Carl (carrl *sic*): man, fellow (Scottish)

Chee-chee: half-caste

Chubbarow: be quiet! Shut up! (from Hindustani)

Coggage: paper or litter; mess

Dekko: look! Watch (from Hindustani)

Doolally: sunstroke (from Hindustani, Deolali, a place in India famous for cases of sunstroke)

Gink: foolish man (North American slang)

Gora: horse (from Hindustani)

Grant Road: the prostitute's quarters in Bombay

Grampi: grandfathers

Hussif: sewing-kit

Jildi: quick! hurry up! (from Hindustani)

Kelly's Eye: first class, Number One

Lariat: a rope used as a lasso, or for tethering

Mallam: do you understand? (from Hindustani)

Matlow: sailor (from French, *matelot*)

Miölnir: Thor's hammer, legendary weapon

Moost: mad, beserk (from Hindustani)

Mutti: sun-baked mud

Napoo: British WWI era army slang meaning 'finished', 'gone'

North: mouth (rhyming slang, *North and south*)

Nullah: waterbed, ravine

Pawny: water (from Hindustani)

Peechi: presently (from Hindustani)

Piard: yellow dog (corruption of pariah)

Pugaree: a scarf wound around the helmet, often worn by the British army abroad

Sexton: an official of the church, sometimes charged with burying the dead

Sidekicker: friend; companion

Soor: swine (from Hindustani: a far worse insult than its English equivalent)

Tap: sunstroke

Tit-fer: hat (rhyming slang, *tit-for-tat*)

Topee: pith helmet

In *The Somme* and its companion *The Coward*, first published in 1927, the heroics of war and noble self-sacrifice are completely absent; replaced by the gritty realism of life in WWI for the ordinary soldier, and the unflinching portrayal of the horrors of war.

Written under the guidance of the master storyteller H. G. Wells, they are classics of the genre. *The Somme* revolves around a futile attack in 1916 during the Somme campaign. Everitt, the central protagonist is wounded and moved back through a series of dressing stations to the General Hospital at Rouen. Both in and out of the line he behaves selfishly and unheroically, but despite this his circumstances and the conditions around him make his actions easy to understand. Based on A. D. Gristwood's own wartime experiences, critics have said that few other accounts of the war give such an accurate picture of trench life. *The Coward* concerns a man who shoots himself in the hand to escape the war, during the March 1918 retreat – an offence punishable by death. He gets away with it, but is haunted by fear of discovery and self-loathing.

April 2016 | ISBN 9781612003801

THE SOMME

ALSO INCLUDING THE COWARD
A. D. Gristwood

Towards the end of the war as the Germans are in their final retreat in November 1918, a British raiding party stumbles across a strange and eerie scene in a ruined chateau, under fire. Following the strains of a familiar tune, and understandably perplexed as to who would be playing the piano in the midst of shellfire, they discover a German officer lying dead at the keys, next to a beautiful woman in full evening dress, also deceased. But the officer is the spitting image of G. B. Bretherton, a British officer missing in action. So follows a tale of mystery and identity which is an authentic account of conditions at the Front.

First published in 1930 this remarkable thriller, with a highly unusual plot, won *Bretherton* comparisons to John Buchan and the best of the espionage writers. John Squire, the influential editor of the *London Mercury* said 'of the English war-books, undoubtedly the best is *Bretherton*.' The *Morning Post* thought it 'one of the best of the English war novels. I do not expect anything much better.' *The Sunday Times* pinpointed its dual attraction: it was both 'a mystery as exciting as a good detective story and an extraordinarily vivid account of trench-warfare'.

April 2016 | ISBN 9781612003764

BRETHERTON
KHAKI OR FIELD-GREY?
W. F. Morris

UNDER FIRE

Henri Barbusse

Set in early 1916, *Under Fire* follows a squad of French volunteer soldiers through the eyes of an unnamed foot soldier, who participates in and also observes the action. It combines soaring, poetic descriptions with the mundane, messy, human reality of soldiers living in their own excrement. Then slowly names and features are given to the men who emerge from the mud, from the dignified leader Corporal Bertrand, to the ebullient Volpatte and the obsessive Cocon. Intermingled with details of how they navigate daily life in the putrified atmosphere of the trenches are both harrowing descriptions and a political, pacifist argument about this war and war more generally.

Caught up in events they cannot control, the soldiers go through their daily routines: foraging for food, reading letters from wives and mothers, drinking, fighting in battle, and in heavily realistic scenes which the novel is noted for, discovering dead bodies in advanced stages of decomposition; the human detritus of a brutal conflict. Through it all, they talk about the war, attempting to make sense of the altered world in which they find themselves. *Under Fire* drew criticism at the time of its publication for its harsh realism, but won the Prix Goncourt. The original translation by Fitzwater Wray which first appeared in 1917 is published here. It captures the essence of the era; a glossary is also provided to help with unfamiliar vocabulary.

April 2016 | ISBN 9781612003825